P9-CRG-176

The Freshman Detective Blues

Also by P. J. Petersen

THE BOLL WEEVIL EXPRESS
CORKY AND THE BROTHERS COOL
GOING FOR THE BIG ONE
GOOD-BYE TO GOOD OL' CHARLIE
HERE'S TO THE SOPHOMORES
NOBODY ELSE CAN WALK IT FOR YOU
WOULD YOU SETTLE FOR IMPROBABLE?

P. J. Petersen

THE FRESHMAN DETECTIVE BLUES

DELACORTE PRESS / NEW YORK

Published by
Dell Publishing
a division of
The Bantam Doubleday Dell Publishing Group, Inc.
666 Fifth Avenue
New York, New York 10103

Manufactured in the United States of America

Library of Congress Cataloging in Publication Data

Petersen, P. J.
The freshman detective blues.

Summary: Eddie, age fourteen, and Jack, age seventeen, find a skeleton weighted down in Muir Lake, and Jack thinks it just might be his father who's been missing for nine years.
[1. Mystery and detective stories] I. Title.
PZ7.P44197Fr 1987 [Fic] 87-5380
ISBN 0-385-29586-3

November 1987

10 9 8 7 6 5 4 3 2

BG

For Marian Braun,
who has always shared her mysteries with me

1

I didn't plan on becoming a detective. And I certainly didn't plan on falling in love. But when you're a freshman in high school, plenty of things happen to you that you don't plan on.

On an ordinary Monday, the twenty-eighth of January, I suddenly found myself (1) in love, (2) in the detective business, and (3) confused about both those things.

The love part happened first. I came out of my algebra class, still in a daze over negative numbers, and crashed into Wendy Westfall, sending her books flying. Now I've known Wendy since kindergarten, but something happened to me while I was gathering her books. I started grinning like an idiot, and I couldn't keep my eyes off her.

The whole thing was crazy. This was old Wendy Westfall, who had been the toughest tetherball player at Ponderosa Elementary School. The girl who had shinnied to the top of the flagpole when we were seventh graders. She was cute and funny, of course—always had been—but it hadn't seemed important before. Then, after one collision in the hall, I couldn't look at her without my heart hammering and my stomach doing somersaults. I walked with her to her Spanish class, grinning all the way.

I needed help. That afternoon, while my friend Jack Mason and I headed across Muir Lake, I decided to ask him for advice. After all, he was seventeen—three years older than I was—and the girls at our school loved him.

It was hard to get the conversation started, though, and Jack's mind was on other things. Our boat, the old aluminum job we used for knocking around, seemed to be the only one on the lake—for good reason. The sky was dark and overcast, and an icy wind was blowing from the south, stirring up gray waves that rose as high as my head. "It'd better not rain," Jack shouted over the noise of the outboard engine.

Jack was probably the only person in the county who wasn't praying for rain that day. We were in the middle of the worst drought anybody could remember. The lake was at its lowest point since the dam had been built back in the 1940s. Looking toward shore, I could see dozens of little islands that hadn't been there a few months before.

Muir Lake, being man-made, always rose and fell during the year. The so-called experts at the dam controlled the flow of water so that the farmers downstream could irrigate their crops and the power commission could generate electricity all year. If everything went right, maybe the resort owners like my parents would have enough water to keep the tourists happy.

In the fall the lake always dropped a hundred feet or so, leaving an ugly red scar between the waterline and the manzanita bushes up above. But last year the lake hadn't filled, and the scar was there through the hot months. During the fall the lake level kept sinking and sinking until now the boat ramp at our place was standing high and dry.

"Let's try it up there," Jack shouted, pointing toward an inlet.

I steered the boat to the right, between two islands. I hoped there was still a channel left. Jack and I had already lost two propellers that winter in places just like that.

I eased back on the throttle. "Check it out."

Jack scooted forward and rested his chin on the bow. "Move it, Eddie," he yelled. "Plenty of water." I gave the throttle a hard twist, and the boat shot forward. Jack glanced back and added, "I think."

"Keep your eyes on the water," I yelled.

He waved me on. "Crank it up. We've got business up ahead."

Jack was a born scrounge. He loved easy money, even if he had to work twice as hard to get it. He was forever looking for something he could fix up and sell.

The drought had opened up a new world for him. All around us lake bottom that had been fifty feet underwater was now dry land. And all the things that had been dropped into the water over the years were out there for the picking—if you didn't mind plowing through the mud.

Jack didn't mind at all. He was like a little kid hunting Easter eggs. I would pull the boat into a cove, and he would leap onto the land and dash along the water's edge, looking for telltale signs. In no time he would be holding on to a piece of monofilament fishing line, following it along in hopes of finding a bass plug at the end.

While we hunted for lures, we kept our eyes peeled for other things. In the garage at Jack's house we had a cardboard box full of tools—wrenches and pliers mostly—cleaned up and ready to take to the flea market when we had time. We also had fishing poles, anchors, ice chests, and tackle boxes that we were saving for next summer's tourists.

Of course, we ran across plenty of things that weren't worth hauling home—old tires, broken beach umbrellas, shoes. We had even found a couple of refrigerators.

Every time we went out, we were hoping to come across something really valuable—maybe one of the aluminum canoes that the old-timers claimed had been lost in the lake. Or another gold bracelet like the one a fisherman had found two weeks before. In the meantime, we picked up lures, worth a dollar or two if they were still solid.

Jack was wearing a pair of size fourteen boots that he had bought at the flea market for a quarter. They were so big he could pull them on over his tennis shoes. And the extra size made them almost like snowshoes for scooting over the top of the mud. Naturally he'd get hung up now and then and have to step out of those boots and pull them out after him.

That day I spent most of my time in the boat. I stayed

even with Jack while he trotted along the shoreline. He used a stick to poke into the mud, but with those clouds overhead we were in too big a hurry to do much digging.

I wasn't too interested in treasure that day anyway. "Hey, Jack," I called out as I putted along, "do you think a person can fall in love in a split second? You know, one minute he's not in love, and the next he is."

Jack poked into a mound with his stick. "Sure."

"Did it ever happen to you?"

"Not more than forty or fifty times. Why?"

"I'm not talking about just thinking somebody's pretty. I mean, really over the edge—like being hit in the stomach with a bowling ball."

"Make it thirty times." He bent over and dug into the mud. He pulled out a rusty can and tossed it aside.

"I'm serious," I said.

"So am I. I'm an emotional guy. Two summers ago, while I was handling the gas pumps, I fell in love with a girl from Loganville, asked her to go steady, decided we were wrong for each other, and broke up with her—all in one afternoon. And I pumped over four hundred gallons of gas besides."

"It's no joke. I'm not even sure I want to be in love. I mean, what if I am? What can I do about it? She lives almost as far from town as we do, so I can't take her anywhere without a car. We have different schedules, so I can't even eat lunch with her. The only place I can see her is in algebra."

"That song you're singing is the freshman blues," Jack said.

"What do I do?"

"Take two aspirin and wait two years."

"I should have known better than to ask you," I said.

"Just take it as it comes. Falling in love hurts sometimes, but you don't die from it."

"I thought you only loved Julie. That's what you always tell her." Julie was my sister, probably the most popular girl in our high school. She and Jack had something going, but I couldn't figure out what. They seemed to be in love, but they both went out with other people. And neither of them ever seemed to be jealous. It didn't seem natural to me.

"There's love, and then there's *love.* Those other thirty, they were love. Julie—she's different." He waved his stick in the air. "That's the stars-in-the-sky, rockets-exploding, heartbreaking, soul-shaking real enchilada."

"I wish I had a pencil," I said. "I'd like to write that down and use it sometime."

"You'd never be able to say it right." He glanced my way. "So who are you in love with this week?"

"Wendy Westfall," I said. "And what's this 'this week' business? I've never been in love before."

"What about Marcie?"

"It's not the same thing."

Jack laughed. "It never is."

"I don't want to talk about it," I said.

Jack kicked at a squarish mound. "I can tell. That's why you brought it up."

"I changed my mind. I don't need advice from somebody who's dumb enough to be in love with my sister."

Jack trotted up the bank. "This place is looking like a dry hole. Why don't you scoot ahead and see if you spot anything worth a look? If you don't, we'll go up past Prentice Point and try it there."

I twisted the throttle and steered the boat away from the bank. Far above me I could see the green and silver of the trees. I loved the lake in the winter—the foggy colors, the ducks in the coves, and the quiet.

I made a quick run up the inlet, then circled back. I beached the boat once to check a mound. Under four inches of mud was a full jar of pickles. I rinsed it off and took it along to show Jack.

"Hey," I called to him, "are you hungry?"

"I was born hungry."

"Have a pickle." I held up the jar as he climbed into the boat.

"They look all right." He pulled off his boots and dipped them over the side to get rid of the mud.

"You can have 'em. I'm too much in love to eat." I wound up the motor and headed the boat back toward the middle of the lake. "Find anything?"

"A couple of lures. One's a big Super Duper. Some dummy had about a three-ounce weight on it. No wonder he got it tangled on the bottom. The other one's chewed up pretty bad. Probably not worth keeping." He looked back at me. "But I kept it anyway."

"That's the story of your life," I said. "You ready to head on back?"

"We'd better hunt while we can," he said. "I don't like the looks of those clouds. This may be our last chance."

"Did you bring a flashlight? You're going to need it."

Jack stretched out in the bottom of the boat. "So tell me about your love life. We've got two or three minutes before we get around the point. That ought to be plenty of time."

"So take a dive overboard," I said.

Prentice Point, an outcropping of dark rock that summer boaters often tie up to, was high above us and a good hundred yards from the shoreline. The land in between looked like a plowed field, with those little humps that the water makes as it slowly moves down.

"Head into the cove," Jack said as I edged the boat toward shore. "When I start getting the right vibrations, we'll stop."

"What is this? You using magic now?"

"You bet, buddy. You've heard of water witches—finding water with their little forked sticks. I'm a junk witch."

We passed some long stretches of muddy beach before he yelled for me to pull into the bank. "You getting vibrations?" I asked.

"Loud and clear." The boat crunched against the bank. Jack stepped out, then shoved the boat free.

I putted along, watching the shoreline while he zigzagged up and down the bank. The sun disappeared from the tops of the trees on the hills above us, and darkness began to settle in. I knew better than to tell Jack it was time to quit. If I did, he'd stay out a few extra minutes just to get a rise out of me.

"Pay dirt," he yelled. He dropped to his knees and began digging. "I told you I was a junk witch."

I eased the boat up against the shore but didn't get out. "What are you finding?"

"It's a motor," he called back. "A good-size one." He kept clawing at the mud.

"Forget it," I said. "It's not worth digging out."

"We'll see. It might not be too bad off."

"Right. Nothing like twenty years in the lake to make a motor run like a champ."

He kept digging all the same. I sat in the boat and thought about Wendy, wondering how I could get her out to the marina for a boat ride.

"This is funny," Jack called. "This thing's got wires wrapped around it."

"I still won't trade you for my pickles."

Jack kept scraping away mud and yanking at the motor. "You could help if you wanted."

"I'd hate to get in the way," I said.

"It's an old Evinrude," he said after some more digging.

"I'll still keep my pickles."

"Hey, you know where this came from?"

"The bottom of the lake."

"It came from the marina. It has *GCM* scratched on the top." That was my home—Grizzly Creek Marina. Woody, the manager, engraved those initials on everything that wasn't nailed down.

"How bad is it?" I asked him.

"Pretty bad. It's rusted out all over. I don't think it's worth hauling home."

"Then leave it," I told him. "It's getting late."

"Just a minute. I want to see what else is here."

I leaned back in the boat and watched him dig. A flock of ducks winged its way into the inlet, saw us, and settled in the water farther up.

"Here you go." Jack threw something toward the boat. "Make yourself useful and wash that off."

I scooted the boat up next to the shore and stepped out. Holding the boat rope in one hand, I scrambled up the bank and picked up what Jack had tossed toward me. It was a license plate, caked with mud. "Keep digging," I said. "Maybe there's a car down there. Or a trailer."

"Listen," Jack said, "there's more than one boat trailer sitting in this lake."

"Not two miles from a boat ramp." I squatted beside the water and scrubbed the red mud off the license. "It's a California plate—three-seven-nine JMG." I cleaned off the upper border and found some renewal stickers still in place. "Not as bad as I thought. According to the stickers, that motor's only been in the water nine years." Jack didn't answer. "Hey, junk witch, how much do you figure we can get for an old license?"

Jack was bent over the hole, digging with both hands.

"What are you doing, Jack? Looking for another valuable license plate?"

He kept digging. "This is weird," he muttered. "This is really weird."

"What is it?" I tossed the license plate into the boat and climbed the bank as far as I could without letting go of the rope. "What are you finding?"

Jack looked down at me. "Bones."

"What do you mean?"

"I mean bones." He was digging with a stick now instead of his hands.

"What's the big deal?"

"I'm not talking about deer bones," Jack said, still digging. "There's a skeleton here. A human skeleton."

"Come on. How can you tell it's human? It's probably—"

"There's a skull here. Come see for yourself."

I let go of the boat rope and dashed up the bank. I took one look into the hole, then spun around and headed down the bank.

Jack laughed. "Where you going?"

"I don't want to have to swim after the boat." I grabbed the rope again.

"Sure," he said.

"We'd better leave it," I told him. "The police won't want us messing up things. You know what they always say on the TV shows: 'Don't touch anything.' "

Jack stood up and turned away from me, looking out toward the lake. I glanced in that direction, but there was nothing to see except the lake, getting darker by the minute.

Then I had a thought. "This is great. Maybe there'll be a reward. If nothing else, we ought to get our picture in the paper." I thought of Wendy Westfall cutting out my picture and pinning it on her bulletin board. "We'll be heroes."

"Yeah." Jack headed up the bank a few steps, grabbed a piece of driftwood, and dragged it down to where he had been digging. He hauled down three more pieces, placing each one over the hole. Then he tromped down to the water's edge. "Let's go home."

"I'm ready." I took a good look around to be sure I could find the spot again, then stepped into the boat.

I was worried as we headed across the dark lake. I could still spot anything above the water, but a rock or a log six inches below the surface would finish us off.

Jack sat in front of me, saying nothing. I figured he was a little spooked by the skeleton. *I* was spooked, and I hadn't had those bones in my hands.

"You okay, Jack?" I called out.

He waved me away.

I left him alone. I had problems of my own—like deciding which shirt to wear when the newspaper people came to take my picture.

When the lights from the marina came into view, I reached forward and gave Jack a push. "Who do we call first—the sheriff or the newspaper?"

Jack swung his legs around and faced me. The boat rocked with his shifting weight, and I cut back on the engine a little.

"Listen, Eddie," he said, "I don't want to call anybody yet, all right?"

"What are you talking about?"

"I don't want to get in a hurry."

"What's the problem? We call up the paper and the sheriff. Then we end up being heroes and getting our picture in the paper."

"Cut the engine," Jack said.

I gave the throttle a twist, and we slowed to trolling speed. "What's wrong?"

"The body was tied to the motor with wire," Jack said.

"You mean?"

"Yeah. Somebody wanted that body to sink and stay sunk."

"Wow." This was even better. I couldn't wait until Wendy found out I was a figure in a murder case.

"So this is weird stuff," Jack said.

"I'll bet there *will* be a reward," I said.

"Forget that stuff, Eddie."

"What's the matter? Don't you want to split with me?"

Jack shoved me, hard. "Will you shut up and listen? This is serious. Think about that license plate. You know what happened around here nine years ago?"

"Yeah," I said, "I started kindergarten."

"Just shut up a second." He took a deep breath and blew it out. "Nine years ago my old man disappeared. And nobody's seen him or heard from him since."

"Oh, man. And you figure—"

"That's right," Jack said. "I think we just found Daddy."

2

I kicked the engine out of gear and looked at Jack. The nose of the boat began to turn with the wind, and we bobbed up and down on the waves.

I couldn't remember what Jack's father had looked like. The only clear memory I had was of his pinkie ring—a fat gold band with a square green stone. I had been fascinated by that ring and had spent most of a summer making rings out of aluminum foil or copper wire.

"Wait a minute," I said. "That could be anybody."

"Maybe," Jack said. "But the motor came from the marina. You know anybody else around there that disappeared just then?"

I glanced toward the marina lights. "So what do you want to do?"

"Maybe we ought to have a little coming-home party." Jack let out a nasty laugh. "All these years I've been waiting for the old man to show up, and he finally made it."

"Come on," I said.

Jack laughed again. "Oh, Daddy, you've lost weight."

"That's sick."

He gave me a shove. "What do you want, Eddie? You want me to cry a little? Feel bad for poor old Daddy? Forget it. I remember that sucker. Rotten clear through. My mother used to tell me to pray for him, and I did. I prayed for him never to come back."

I put the engine in gear. "We'd better go in. Woody's going to be having a cow."

"I'm ready," Jack said.

"You're sure you don't want to call the cops?"

"Let's poke around ourselves and see what we can find out. Do our own detective work."

"But what if we don't find out anything?"

"Just trust me, all right?"

I twisted the throttle, and the nose of the boat lifted off the water. I really didn't believe any of it. This was Muir Lake—Grizzly Creek Marina—home sweet home. Dead bodies didn't belong here.

While we were plowing through the waves, the rest of the problem began to sink in. Somebody had dumped that body out there. So there was a killer somewhere. And that killer was somebody who could get hold of a motor from our marina.

Ahead of us were the lighted docks, a giant *E* with the three legs pointing toward the open water. Most of the locals moored their boats at the marina, and we were always full, with a waiting list. I circled around the north side of the docks and eased our boat into its slip.

Woody Hall was already stomping down the docks toward us. "Grandma Woody's on the warpath," Jack said.

Woody was only about fifty, but I always thought of him as a little old man—or sometimes as a little old lady. A born grump, he always looked as if he had been sucking a lemon.

"I was about ready to call the sheriff," he said. He had one hand on his straw hat to keep it from flying. He was bald as an egg, so he never took off that hat.

"Don't worry about us," I called back.

"I don't care about you two, but I don't want to lose my boat." Actually the boat and the whole marina belonged to my family; but Woody was in charge of everything on the water, and he never let us forget it. "Clean up that thing now. I'm tired of having you leave it full of mud."

"We'll do it tomorrow," I said, knowing we wouldn't. That aluminum boat was light enough so that Jack and I could haul it out of the water and scrub it down. We planned to do that one of these days. In the meantime, the mud didn't hurt anything. Nobody was going to rent it in the winter anyway.

Woody snorted. "What's the matter with you two? You too dumb to quit when it gets dark?"

We didn't pay any attention. Woody talked that way to everybody, including his best customers.

The three of us walked back toward the store. The dock beneath our feet creaked and moaned as it swayed with the waves. "Think it's going to rain?" I asked Woody.

He shrugged. "I've been thinking it's going to rain for six months."

Woody's store was small and cluttered, but it had what boat people needed—groceries, cold drinks, fishing gear, and gasoline. Woody did a good business in spite of the high prices and the rotten service. He might growl at you, but he was always open, and he knew where the fish were biting.

The only person inside was Pooch Wexler, doing push-ups in the aisle by the freezer. Pooch was past seventy, but his body was solid. And he still had a full head of shaggy white hair—a fact he was always pointing out to Woody.

"Here come the junkmen," Pooch said, bouncing to his feet. He was wearing his usual jeans and T-shirt.

"Go home if you gotta exercise," Woody said. "This place stinks like a gym." Pooch's houseboat was moored at the far end of the middle dock, but he spent a good part of his time around the store, getting on Woody's nerves. Woody was a hundred-words-a-day man who did everything according to a system; Pooch was a motor mouth with no system at all. That combination was good for two or three fights a week.

Pooch had his eye on the paper bag Jack was carrying. "Whatcha got today?"

Jack reached into the bag. "Got a nice Super Duper."

Pooch began to smile. "Let's see it."

Woody snorted. "You dumb old fool, you need another lure like you need another hole in your head."

"It's not nice to call names, you bald-headed toad." Pooch ran his fingers through his hair. "Besides, who said I was gonna buy it? I just want to see it."

Jack dangled the Super Duper in front of Pooch. "It's a beauty. Probably got lost on the first cast. Go ahead. Make me an offer I can't refuse."

It didn't seem right to me. Jack had just dug up his father, and he was carrying on the way he always did.

Woody moved behind the counter. "You boys want anything?" When we shook our heads, he opened the cash register and began stacking the coins—something he had learned from my grandfather. He examined each one quickly, always on the lookout for old ones or silver ones. Grandpa had done the same kind of checking every night, year after year. And he had ended up with a whale of a coin collection to show for it.

"I'll give you fifty cents for that thing," Pooch said to Jack.

Jack swung the lure back and forth. "That's okay for rent. I thought you wanted to buy it, though."

"Seventy-five, and be glad you got it."

"It's brand-new," Jack said.

The pay phone outside the store rang. We all knew it was Opal, Woody's mother, calling to say that dinner was ready. Pooch scooted out the door and picked up the receiver on the second ring. "Joe's Pool Hall." He laughed once, then said, "How's everything going, sweetheart? You getting a little lonesome up there? Maybe I ought to come up tonight and—" He laughed and set down the receiver. "She says dinner'll be ready in five minutes. If you're too busy, I could go up and eat it for you."

Woody nodded and started dumping the coins into white bank bags.

"You tell your mother she's gonna hurt my feelings hanging up on me like that. Tell her a lady should have better manners."

Woody moved out from behind the counter. "You guys get moving. I got supper waiting."

Jack and I headed out the door. "It's a rough life, boys," Pooch said. "Woody goes home to a big steak and a baked potato, and I go down to my boat and open a can of SpaghettiOs."

Woody flipped off the lights, activated the burglar alarm, and locked the door.

"I'll give you a buck for that Super Duper," Pooch told Jack, "and that's my final offer." He looked disappointed when Jack handed him the lure without an argument. "I'll pay you later."

"We're running a cash business," Jack said.

Pooch grinned and pulled a crumpled dollar bill out of his pants pocket. "You've got a bad attitude. Been hanging around bald guys too long."

Jack and I followed Woody across the aluminum walkway that led to shore. Woody's pickup was sitting at the bottom of the boat ramp. We hopped into the back and got a ride.

The resort always looked like a ghost town in the winter, but that night the empty parking lots and the dark buildings looked creepy—like the set of a horror movie.

I leaned toward Jack and whispered, "Let's call the sheriff."

"We made a deal. Now shut up."

Woody slowed down as he passed our mailbox, and I hopped off. I stood in the road and watched the pickup until it made a right turn into Woody's driveway. Jack vaulted over the side and headed up the road toward his house. "See you later," I yelled. He waved without turning back.

The upper half of Grizzly Creek Marina was spread over five acres of pines. Next to the road and overlooking the docks was our restaurant, the Pelican's Perch. It looked like a log cabin with picture windows. Our house, which also looked like a log cabin, sat in a clearing behind the restaurant. The rental cabins were scattered in the trees between our house and the lake.

Walking up the gravel driveway, I kept glancing over at the Pelican's Perch. The place was dark, of course. In the winter we opened it only for wedding receptions and private parties. But I heard scraping sounds, and I felt somebody watching me.

Then a shape appeared above the peak of the roof. I jumped behind a tree.

Ricky Batt pointed a stick in my direction and yelled, "Bang, bang, you're dead. Three bullets in your head."

My heart was doing about two hundred beats a minute. If Ricky had known that, it would have made his day. I caught my breath and yelled, "Get down from there."

Ricky and Tony Batt, called the Batt brats by everybody but their parents, had been terrorizing the resort ever since they had moved in last fall. Their mother, Barbara, was a cousin of Mom's. She had talked Mom into letting them stay in one of the tourist cabins temporarily, even though the cabins weren't equipped for winter use.

Before a week had passed, Dad and Woody wanted to send the Batts packing. Softhearted Mom defended them until the day Tony got stuck in our chimney. (I think they were playing Santa Claus.)

The Batts were supposed to be looking for another place to live, but I don't think they were looking too hard.

Meanwhile, Barbara worked all day at a health food store in Los Cedros, and her husband, Roger, was supposed to watch the brats. But Roger was also trying to work on his sculpture, which involved making a big piece of rusty junk out of little pieces of rusty junk. Once Roger started welding, he forgot about everything else, and the brats went off on another search-and-destroy mission.

"You're dead meat," Ricky yelled.

"Get off that roof."

Ricky stood up. "Make me, stupid."

Tony's head popped up. "Make me, stupid."

"I don't care." I walked a few steps up the driveway. "Say hi to the screech owl for me."

"There's no screech owl up here," Ricky called back. Tony scooted out of sight.

"Just stand still when he flies past," I said. "That way he usually won't bite."

"Liar," Ricky yelled. "Liar, liar, pants on fire."

I think he was already on the way down, but his mother showed up before I could be sure.

"That's not how we talk, Ricky," she said in the quiet voice she always used.

Tony came running. "Hi, Mommy salami," he yelled. Barbara scooped him up with one arm and pulled him close. A second later Ricky was buried in the other arm.

"Eddie," Barbara said, "I have some capsules for

your mom." Still holding the boys, she came toward me and handed over a paper bag. "I think they might help that elbow of hers."

Barbara was always bringing people things like alfalfa tablets or yeast cakes. My mother always thanked her, and the stuff disappeared. Probably down the toilet, but Mom would never admit it.

"How's your complexion doing these days, Eddie?"

I happened to have three zits that day—I had counted. But that wasn't information I cared to make public. "It's okay."

"If you start having trouble, let me know. I have some wonderful stuff that'll clear up your face in no time."

"Mommy," Ricky said, "is there a screech owl up on that roof?"

Barbara laughed and started back toward their cabin. "I don't think so," she said. "I think the buzzard and the bats chased it away."

"I'm back," I called as I came through the door. I wondered if I'd be able to keep the secret. My family has always been able to read my face like a book.

But at the dinner table that night, nobody even looked at me. Dad had just beaten Barney Hamilton in racquetball, and he gave us a play-by-play of the match. Mom kept glancing out the window, watching for signs of rain. Julie got three phone calls and ate most of her meal standing up.

After helping with the dishes and staring at my homework for a while, I slipped out of the house and headed for the docks. I wanted some privacy when I called Wendy.

Our driveway seemed darker than usual. I knew it was silly, but I kept looking around as I walked. Then something rustled in the trees overhead. That was enough for me. I took off running and didn't stop until I made it to the bottom of the boat ramp.

Conditions at the marina weren't exactly ideal for a romantic conversation. The wind was howling, and the docks groaned as they rose and fell. Even so, it was better than trying to talk with Julie around.

I got out my money, then tried to think of an opening line. I didn't want to get Wendy on the line and go into a stammering fit. I thought about asking for help on the algebra homework, but I hadn't done my problems yet. I decided to tell her I had lost the assignment. That wouldn't win any prizes for originality, but it was a way to get started.

When I finally shoved my money in the slot, I misdialed, started over, and misdialed again. On the third try I got the number right, but the line was busy.

I spent the next half hour dropping in my money, dialing, and listening to the blat of the busy signal. Between tries I huddled in the doorway of the store and thought about those muddy bones out beyond Prentice Point.

I dropped in my money for about the fortieth time and dialed carefully. After four clicks and a pause the same sickening blats started again.

A hand clamped down on my shoulder. "What are you up to?"

I dropped the receiver and jerked away. I took two steps, then spun around, my hands in front of my face.

Pooch Wexler let out a cackle. "You're a little nervous

tonight, Eddie." He was standing there in his swimming trunks, a towel thrown over his shoulder.

"Oh, man, you scared me to death."

Pooch kept laughing like an idiot. "I wish you could have seen the look on your face."

"What do you expect? You come sneaking up on me that way."

"You jumped like a rattler bit you." He reached over and hung up the telephone. "What's the matter, Eddie? Can't get Julie off your home phone?"

"How'd you guess?" I watched the wind blow his white hair around his face. "Aren't you cold?"

"Of course. That's the whole point. The cold's good for you. Improves your circulation. A little swim, and your whole body gets pumping."

"You're not really going in, are you? That water's freezing."

"You've just gotta be tough, Eddie. I was just getting ready to jump in when I saw somebody down here and thought I'd better check."

"No burglar this time," I said. I thought about the motor Jack had found that afternoon and decided it was the perfect time for some detective work. "We don't have much problem with stuff getting stolen around here, do we?"

"Not with the Silver Fox on duty," Pooch said. "I keep telling Woodrow he ought to pay me a night watchman's salary, but you know how far I get with that."

"What's the biggest thing that ever got stolen anyway?"

Pooch grinned. "I don't know, but whatever it was,

those Batt brats probably got it. You never saw shoplifters like those two in your life. That first day, Woody grabbed the little one and emptied out his pants and shirt. Little rascal had enough stuff to fill a shopping bag. And he palmed three packs of gum while Woody was lecturing him."

"I mean big stuff," I said. "You suppose anybody ever stole a boat? Or a motor?"

"I doubt it. Too many lights here. Too much going on."

"Seems like a guy could come down here in the middle of the night and help himself."

"Shoot," Pooch said, "Woodrow's got everything tied down, boarded up, and padlocked. Besides, no burglars are gonna tangle with me. The Silver Fox would chew 'em up and spit 'em out." He snapped me on the leg with the towel. "You want to do me a favor?"

"As long as it doesn't cost anything."

He tossed me the towel. "Carry that over to my boat. I'll hop in here and swim back."

"You're nuts," I said.

"Just tough, that's all." He stepped between two boats and dived into the water. He surfaced and let out a yelp. "Hoo-eee. That'll get you hopping." Then he began a slow crawl in the direction of his houseboat.

I walked along the dock, carrying the towel. I felt like a dope. Pooch was the biggest gossip in the country. Even a crummy detective should have been able to learn something from him. But not me.

When he scrambled up the ladder into his boat, I tossed him the towel. "You don't know what you're missing, Eddie boy."

"I can do without pneumonia."

"Bunch of sissies around here," he yelled.

I headed back to the telephone. The line stayed busy until I gave up, and then I got spooked on the way back and ended up running home.

And I couldn't do the algebra problems either.

3

I didn't sleep much that night. I kept waking up and looking around my dark room. Sooner or later somebody was going to find out about that skeleton and ask why we hadn't reported it right away. And I was stumped for an answer.

At six o'clock Dad's alarm went off. Five minutes later the front door shut quietly. On weekdays he ran for forty-five minutes, which gave him twenty minutes to shower and dress and be ready to eat at seven-ten.

Everything at Grizzly Creek Marina was like that. Lying there in bed at ten after six, I knew where Dad would be on the road. And I knew that fifty yards through the pines from our house Woody and Opal would be sitting at the table, their television tuned to the early-morning news. And fifty yards beyond that Louise Mason (Jack's mom) would be frosting the cinnamon rolls that Woody sold in his store every morning. For a minute I thought about skipping out of my warm bed and trotting over to Jack's for one of those rolls.

Even the Batts were predictable. Barbara and Roger would still be asleep. She didn't leave for the health food store until after nine, so she had another hour before she got up and fixed tofu cakes for breakfast. Meanwhile, the brats were probably putting together a bomb or removing each other's tonsils.

Every morning was the same, everybody following the old routine. But now I knew that things weren't as simple as they seemed. Out past Prentice Point was a skeleton, and the chances were good that somebody around the marina had put it there.

At seven-ten we sat down to a breakfast of twelve-grain cereal, a kind of oatmeal glop that Barbara had given my mother. The stuff wasn't too bad once you quit expecting it to have any taste. But it was a far cry from one of Louise Mason's cinnamon rolls.

Dad left for his job at the lumberyard at seven-thirty, and Julie disappeared into the bathroom. I gathered my books and wandered out to the kitchen, where Mom was having a second cup of coffee.

"I thought Barbara had gotten you to switch to herbal tea," I said.

Mom shook her head. "I gave it a shot, but I just couldn't face rose hips and camomile in the morning."

The clock over the stove clicked to seven forty-seven. I glanced out the window. Any second now Jack's pickup would show up in our driveway. First period at Los Cedros High began at eight-thirty. From the marina it was a five-minute drive up Grizzly Creek Road to the main highway, then a twenty-minute drive into town. If Julie was ready to go, we'd have time to hit our lockers and still make it to class before the last bell. But she was never ready on time.

"Sure looks like rain," I said.

Mom sighed. "I'll believe it when I see it."

"Hey, Mom, what was Jack's father like? Jack was talking about him the other day, but I hardly remember him."

"I'm not surprised. You were only four or five when he left, and he wasn't around here very often."

"Jack says he was a rat."

Mom set down her coffee and smiled. "That's about right. Maybe a little generous."

"Really rotten, huh?"

"To the core." She turned in her chair. "Is that Jack?"

"Yeah." Jack's pickup was halfway up our driveway. "What'd he do?"

"Nothing special. He was just a lousy human being. Don't say anything to Jack, though."

"Come on, Mom. I wouldn't go tell him something like that."

Mom looked toward the bathroom and called, "Julie, Jack's here."

"Just a second," Julie answered. We all knew that was a lie.

I went to the window and waved to Jack. He didn't look like a guy who had just found his father's skeleton. He was leaning back in the seat as usual, tapping his fingers on the steering wheel. That truck was the perfect machine for him. He had built it out of parts from three wrecked pickups. The engine ran beautifully, but the body was a mess—mostly blue, with green doors and one red fender.

Julie fussed about riding in that thing, calling it visual pollution. Of course, she could have gotten up earlier and gone with Dad, but she preferred riding with Jack and fussing.

"Hey!" Jack yelled. He jumped out of the pickup and went dashing across the restaurant parking lot.

"What happened?" Mom asked me.

"I think the Batt brats have struck again," I said, grabbing up my books and my lunch. When I came out the door, Jack was walking back toward me.

"Those little brats threw rocks at my truck," he said. "Then they just stood there with their tongues out, waiting for me to chase them."

"Did you catch 'em?"

"No way." Jack grinned. "Little devils have a crawl hole under the restaurant. You should have heard them giggle."

Mom opened the door and said, "She's coming."

I glanced at my watch. "No hurry. We can still make second period."

"Mrs. Carter," Jack said, "the monsters have figured out how to get underneath the restaurant. Maybe you'd better get them out of there before they start disconnecting the plumbing."

"Maybe we could board up the hole," I said. "With them inside."

Mom sighed. "I'll take care of it."

Julie came out the door and said, "Sorry to keep you waiting," without sounding sorry at all. She was almost as pretty as she thought she was—tall and slim with long, straight hair and sparkling brown eyes. She wore more eye shadow (green) than she needed, but I seemed to be the only one who cared. She had half the boys at Los Cedros High chasing her, and the other half would have chased her if they hadn't figured it was a lost cause.

"If I flunk geography, it's your fault," I told her.

Julie waved good-bye to Mom and slid to the middle of the pickup seat. Jack climbed in beside her and gave her a smile. "The only trouble with seeing you first thing in the morning is that there's nowhere to go from there but down."

"That's a new one," she said. "And a nice one. Thank you."

I planned to remember that line. It might come in handy.

Jack put the truck in gear and started down the driveway. He flipped on the radio, but all we got was the eight o'clock news. I reached for a cassette from the glove compartment.

KA-THUNK. A rock the size of a grapefruit bounced off the hood of the truck. Jack slammed on the brakes. Ricky and Tony stood in the restaurant parking lot, their tongues sticking out. I threw open the door, but the pickup started forward. "I'll get you for that," Jack yelled.

Ricky stuck his thumbs in his ears and waved his fingers.

"That's all right," Jack said, turning onto the road. "I have some welding projects for Roger to do. He can pay for the damage that way."

Grizzly Creek Road was just wide enough for two cars to pass if they both hugged the sides. We met one

Winnebago that forced us to back up to a wide spot. Julie looked at her watch and sighed.

Just before we hit the main highway, we saw Vince Minetti coming toward us. Vince was a sergeant in the sheriff's department, in charge of the whole lake district. He usually stopped by for a cinnamon roll on his way to Los Cedros.

Jack waved for Vince to stop, then jumped out of the pickup. I was curious enough to go with him. "We're going to be late," Julie said.

"What's happening?" Vince asked us, rolling down the window. His huge body took up all the space between the car seat and the steering wheel.

"We found something in the lake yesterday," Jack said.

I felt as if a fifty-pound weight had dropped off my shoulders. I only wished Jack had called the newspaper first.

"What's that?" Vince asked.

"A license plate."

I turned away so that Vince couldn't see my disgusted face.

"Where'd you find it, Jack?"

"On the shoreline, couple miles north." Jack trotted over to the pickup and got the plate from underneath the seat. "Here you go."

Vince looked at the plate but didn't reach for it. "What's the big deal, Jack?"

Jack knelt down beside the door. "I think maybe it came off a Model A."

"What makes you think so?"

"I heard people talking."

Vince laughed. "Fairy tales, Jackie. Who've you been listening to—old Pooch?"

"I know it's a long shot," Jack said, "but I heard that two guys were using a Model A for a brush buggy. It got away from them and went down the bank into a hundred feet of water."

Vince laughed again. "You believe in the Easter bunny too?"

"It's possible," Jack said. "And you know how much Model A parts are worth."

"Somebody's blowing smoke, boy. I've heard those stories for years. There's always a Model A somewhere—up on a mining claim or down in the lake. Only nobody ever finds it."

"How about giving me a break?" Jack said. "How about calling that plate in and seeing if it came off a Model A?"

"Okay," Vince said. "Just because I'm a nice guy. But don't get your hopes up."

"Will you do it now?"

"I'll do it when I get to the office. I don't want to bother the dispatcher. Besides, right now I'm ready for breakfast." Vince wrote down the numbers in his notebook. "What about the tooth fairy, Jack? You believe in him too?"

Jack and I headed back to the truck. "Hurry up," Julie called. "If we're lucky, we can still make it on time."

But we weren't lucky. We ended up behind a logging truck for five miles. By the time we got to school, the parking lot was full of cars and empty of people.

"Here we go again," Julie said, pushing past me and trotting for the door.

"Why hurry now?" I said. "One minute late or five—it doesn't make any difference."

Jack and I were almost to the main door when the final bell rang. "Story of my life," I muttered.

"You feel that?" Jack said.

Before I could answer, a big drop of rain struck the top of my head. Then drops began spotting the sidewalk in front of us. "It's finally coming," I said.

Jack turned toward me. "And that lake's going to start rising."

4

By the time I reached my geography class, the skies had opened up. The whole class was standing by the windows, cheering the end of the drought. Mr. Crowell didn't even see me slip in.

All day the rain battered against the windows and roared out of the downspouts. By noon the parking lot was three inches deep in water. The gutters on each side of the street were brown rivers, washing up over the sidewalks in low spots.

Jack caught me at my locker after fifth period. "Get all your stuff right now," he said. "We'll take off the minute school is out."

"What's the hurry?"

"We're going for a little boat ride."

I looked at him. "In this stuff?"

He leaned against the locker. "Yep. It's our last chance to visit old Dad. The way it's been raining, he'll be underwater before dark." The casual pose didn't fool me—not when his voice kept shaking.

During sixth period the rain turned to hail. When I came out the side door at the end of school, some guys were dashing around the white lawn, scooping up handfuls of hailstones.

Jack and Julie were already in the pickup. I slogged through the water in the parking lot and climbed in. We tore out of the lot, sending water spraying out behind us. A snowball (hailball?) smacked against the windshield.

"See Jack zoom out of school," Julie chanted. "See Jack zoom down the street. See Jack wrap his ugly pickup around a telephone pole."

"We're all right," Jack muttered, but the pickup slowed down.

"I just hope the road is still open," I said.

It was—barely. We crept through flooded sections, crawled around mudslides, and dodged rocks on the pavement.

When we finally reached our driveway, we saw the Batt brats, soaked to the skin, wading in the drainage ditch. Tony looked up long enough to stick out his tongue.

"That's awful," Julie said. "Roger shouldn't let them outside on a day like this."

"Think about poor old Roger," I said. "How would you like to be trapped in a tiny cabin with those two monsters?"

Jack stopped the pickup beside our steps. "See you in five minutes," he said.

"Make it three." I threw open the door and raced for the house.

Mom was at the kitchen table, working on her accounts. "Isn't it wonderful?" she called. "It's been pouring all day. I can't remember the lake ever coming up this fast."

"That's great." I headed straight for my room.

"Don't you want something to eat?"

"I'll get something." I kicked off my shoes. "Jack and I are going down to help Woody." I knew better than to tell her we were going out on the lake.

I put on some grubby clothes and a plastic raincoat, then grabbed a banana and headed for the door.

Julie, sitting at the table with Mom, called out, "Some people don't have sense enough to come in out of the rain."

Jack was standing under a tree at the end of the driveway. He had on his old leather jacket, and he was holding a plastic garbage bag above his head.

"Where'd the brats go?" I asked.

"Behind the restaurant, I think. They took off running when they spotted me."

We trotted down the hill and across the aluminum walkway, which was lurching with the waves. Woody, dressed in his yellow rain clothes, was fussing with the cables. Whenever the lake rose or fell, he had to move the docks accordingly. He always moaned and swore, but he'd never let any of us help much. The docks were his baby.

"We have to go out on the lake," I told him. "How about letting us take something with a top on it?"

"Don't go out there," he said. "It's too rough."

"We'll be careful."

"Idiots." Woody turned his back and started turning the winch.

"Come on. What about number fifteen?"

He kept his back to me. "I've got all those boats cleaned out. I won't have you tracking mud into 'em now."

"Forget it," Jack said. "Let's go." We piled into our old aluminum job and headed out at full throttle.

"So tell me about your love life," Jack shouted over his shoulder.

I was crouched behind him, using his body to block off some of the wind. "Nothing to tell."

"Did you see Wendy today?"

"She was absent. That's the way my luck's going."

"Call her and give her the assignments. Perfect excuse."

"I guess." I scrunched down lower.

Crossing the open stretch of lake was like swimming upstream against the current. I kept the boat pointed in the right direction and tried to hit the waves head-on so that we wouldn't get swamped. We rose with each wave, then crashed down with a thump, just in time for the next one.

Sitting in front, Jack caught more spray than I did, but we were already so wet from the rain that it didn't make much difference.

And the rain kept coming, huge drops rattling down on the aluminum boat and smacking against my face. All along the shore the water had turned chocolate brown with the muddy runoff. The inlets, fed now by the swollen creeks, were a reddish brown—the color of the red clay sidehills.

I leaned forward and shouted, "You know Wayne Parks?"

"Sort of. He's a dip."

"I found out that he likes Wendy. He goes over to her house all the time."

"Wake up, Eddie. If you find a girl that nobody likes, there's probably a reason for it."

"Yeah, but Wayne's a junior with a car."

"And you're a freshman with a bicycle. What's the big deal?"

"Forget it."

Jack smacked my knee. "No reason to worry about a little competition, Eddie. Just because he's got a nice car and he's older and smarter and better-looking—"

"You're a real buddy," I said.

By the time we passed Prentice Point, my stomach was getting rocky from the ride. I kept the throttle wide open as we headed up the inlet. It was good to be away from the worst of the waves.

I had trouble getting my bearings. The rain was so heavy that I couldn't make out the tops of the hills, and the lake had risen far enough to change the appearance of the shoreline. "Hey, Jack," I yelled, "are we getting close?"

"I think so." He reached for his big boots. "Take it slow. Maybe we'll recognize something."

I kept looking for the driftwood that Jack had used to cover the spot, but the rising water and the wind had spread driftwood all along the water's edge. I started watching the lake instead of the shoreline. The last thing we needed right then was to lose a propeller to a floating log.

"This is it," Jack shouted.

Nothing looked familiar to me. "Are you sure?"

"More or less. Turn off the motor, and we'll beach it."

I headed the nose of the boat toward shore, gave the throttle one final twist, then shut off the motor and raised the prop. When the boat smacked against the mud, Jack leaped onto the bank. He grabbed the rope and pulled the boat forward.

"I don't see anything," I said.

Jack headed away from me. "It's gotta be around here."

I stepped onto the slippery bank and hauled the boat as far out of the water as I could. I kept the rope in my hand because there was nothing to tie it to.

I stood and shivered while Jack slogged along the shoreline, working his way up and down the bank. What did I need a skeleton for? I could think of a thousand things—starting with a cup of hot chocolate and a hamburger—that I would rather have had than all the skeletons in the county.

"Here it is," Jack yelled. "This is it." He stepped into the water.

I shoved the boat free and hauled it with me as I tramped along the muddy shoreline. Ten feet from the spot where Jack was wading, I beached the boat again.

"I still don't recognize anything," I said.

Jack slogged deeper into the water. "This is the place. The stuff's already covered up, though."

"Where is it?"

"Brilliant question. If I knew that, would I be wading around out here? But it's— aiee!" His foot sank, and the water poured into his boot. "That's it." He came tromping toward the boat, water flying in all directions.

"Ready to pack it in?" I asked.

"Nope." He plopped down on the muddy bank and pulled off his boots, then his sneakers. "Nice day for a swim anyway."

"Come on," I said. "You're not really going back in there, are you?"

Jack stripped off his jacket and tossed it into the boat. He began fumbling with the buttons on his shirt.

"I don't get it," I said.

"Look, this spot may never be uncovered again. If I decide to call the cops, I want some proof there was a body here. Otherwise they'd laugh us out of the place." He turned toward me. "Give me a hand, will you?"

Even with both of us working, it took a long time to get Jack out of his shirt. Our fingers were too stiff to handle the buttons. He didn't bother about his jeans, which were already soaked anyway.

"See if you can find me a good stick," he said.

I pulled the boat farther up onshore, then dashed around until I found a good straight piece of driftwood. By then Jack was up to his waist in the water, moving slowly back and forth.

"Here you go," I said. I threw the stick like a javelin, missing him by more feet than I'd intended.

"You always were a lousy shot," he yelled.

I huddled next to the boat while he used the stick to probe. Soon the waves were hitting his chest.

"Forget it," I yelled.

"Shut up and leave me alone." He kept moving along in the same regular pattern. His stick jerked up and down, sending water flying. I climbed into the boat and crouched into a ball, my arms wrapped around my knees. The rain beat down on the top of my head.

"Bingo!" Jack yelled.

I looked up in time to see him toss the stick aside. "Whatcha got?"

"Finally hit that motor."

His head disappeared beneath the surface of the brown water. I counted twenty-eight before he came up. He showed me his empty hands.

"Let it go," I yelled.

His head disappeared once more. When he surfaced again, he didn't even look my way.

I stepped onto the bank, pushed the boat free, and hauled it along the shoreline. I wanted to get as close to Jack as possible.

He surfaced, took a couple of deep breaths, and went under again. I didn't bother to yell at him. I just stood and watched the spot where he had been.

One hand came out of the water, then his head. He paddled awkwardly, then stood up. The water came to his chest. For a minute he stayed in the same spot, his mouth wide open as he sucked in air and let it go with grunting moans.

"Can you make it okay?" I yelled.

He took a few steps in my direction, then slipped forward, his face smacking the water. I had ripped off my raincoat and was ready to plunge in when he surfaced again. He got to his feet, then staggered through the shallower water and grabbed on to the boat.

I helped him up onto the bank and then into the boat. He said something, but his jaw was shaking so badly that I couldn't understand him.

I didn't even try to get off his wet clothes. I wrapped his shirt around him, then covered him with his jacket.

He reached into the waistband of his jeans and pulled out a muddy stick. He tried to hand it to me but dropped it into the bottom of the boat. I wouldn't have bothered with it right then, but he pointed and yelled.

I reached down and grabbed it with my shaking fingers. It felt slick. I held it out toward Jack, then realized what it was—a bone. I opened my fingers and let it drop to the bottom of the boat again.

Jack let out a howl and pointed at the bone.

"Great," I said, scooting back toward the engine.

He yelled louder, then pointed at his garbage bag. Then he pointed at me and the bone.

"I get the picture," I said, grabbing the garbage bag. I spent a minute finding the opening, then tried to figure out how to pick up the bone without touching it. Jack started to yell again.

"All right. Just shut up." I snatched up the bone and threw it in the bag. Then I shoved the bag next to Jack's feet. He bobbed his head up and down. "You're not welcome." I reached over the side and rinsed off my hand.

I started the motor and headed the boat back toward the marina. Jack crouched low, ducking his head between his knees.

After taking it easy for a few minutes, I decided I couldn't get any colder. I drew my knees up against my chest and twisted the throttle wide open. While we crashed through the waves, I wondered if I was going to freeze to death. And I wondered if I cared.

When we finally reached the marina, Pooch came out of the store with an umbrella and walked down the dock to our slip. "Hoo-eee," he yelled. "You two look like drowned rats."

Jack staggered onto the dock, the garbage bag in his hand. His jacket slipped off his shoulders, but he didn't seem to notice.

"You look terrible," Pooch said. "I'll tie up for you. You boys get into the store by the heater and get some coffee down you."

I couldn't make my legs work right. My whole body was trembling, and I couldn't manage to climb out of the boat. Pooch finally hauled me out and half carried me to the store. "You boys got some weird ideas about how to spend the afternoon," he muttered.

We must have looked pretty bad. Pooch felt sorry enough for us that he hiked up to our houses in the rain and got us some dry clothes. And he didn't even lecture us or laugh at us.

In fifteen minutes or so I was doing better. I couldn't get warm enough, but I wasn't shaking anymore. Jack stayed hunched over the heater, his hands still trembling.

A little later Woody came marching into the store, water streaming off his yellow rain clothes. He looked at the piles of wet clothes and snorted. "Idiots. What'd you do—go swimming?"

"You bet," I said. "It gets the old blood pumping. Just ask old Pooch here."

"You two don't have the brains you were born with." Woody waved his arm and sent a spray of water in Jack's direction.

Jack didn't look up. He just sat and stared at the garbage bag that lay at his feet.

5

After dinner I ran down to the docks and got soaked again. My big payoff for risking pneumonia was a one-minute conversation with Wendy's mother, who told me that Wendy was asleep and that she already had all her assignments. She didn't tell me that it was a pain and a bother to have me call, but she might as well have.

I put in another rough night. I spent a good part of it watching the lightning and thinking about the muddy bone.

By morning the rain had slacked off to a steady drizzle, and life at the marina dropped back into its usual routine. Dad went for his morning jog and left for work at seven-thirty. While we ate breakfast, the usual cars went by, heading for the marina and the cinnamon rolls. Jack's pickup came down our driveway at ten minutes to eight, and, of course, Julie wasn't quite ready.

Mom sat by the window, watching the Batt brats

slide down the hill behind the restaurant. They were so covered with red mud that you couldn't tell what color clothes they had on—or *if* they had clothes on, for that matter. Mom sipped her coffee and sighed. "I know why young people are parents. At my age I couldn't face two mudballs like that."

If Jack had had a rough night, he didn't show it. He was playing a rock tape and tapping his fingers on the dashboard. When Julie rushed down the steps and climbed into the truck, he had a poem ready for her:

> She walks in beauty, like the night
> Of cloudless climes and starry skies;
> And all that's best of dark and bright
> Meet in her aspect and her eyes. . . .

Julie laughed as she pulled out her comb and tried to fix her windblown hair. "Thanks, Jack. It's not very accurate, but I appreciate the thought."

"You memorized that?" I asked him.

"I tried to, but I gave it up." He showed me the slip of paper in his hand, then put the truck in gear. "I kept forgetting the middle part."

Julie reached over and kissed him on the cheek. "That's sweet."

Jack grinned. "Hey, you've got to work on your aim. You missed my lips by three inches."

We met a steady stream of cars on Grizzly Creek Road. I guess everybody wanted to see how much the lake had risen.

When we reached the main highway, Jack pulled to the shoulder of the road and yanked the emergency brake. "Vince ought to be along any second. I want to talk to him."

"We're cutting it pretty close," Julie said. "Old Miss Vernon is just waiting for me."

Jack held up his watch. "If he isn't here in one minute, we'll go on."

When Vince came along four minutes later, Jack and I hopped out of the truck and trotted over to him.

Vince rolled down the window. "Think it'll rain?"

"Did you call in that plate?" Jack asked, squatting beside the door.

"Yep," Vince said. "Guess what. There ain't no Santa Claus. And there ain't no Model A down there either."

"What is it?" Jack asked.

"It's just a license plate, Jackie. No car attached." Vince dug into his glove compartment and pulled out a slip of paper. "It came off a 1968 Chevy, but don't go getting excited. The Chevy's not down there. Stolen plate probably. Kids are always swiping 'em. Or maybe it fell off."

"That's the way it goes," Jack said. "Was it from around here?"

"Nah. Belonged to some guy in San Francisco." Vince glanced down at the slip. "August Bartolozzi. Willner Street. Frisco."

Jack stood up. "How about giving me that slip for a souvenir? It'll be a good reminder not to get my hopes up."

Vince laughed and crumpled the paper in his hand. "You don't need a reminder, Jackie. If you think I'm gonna let you forget this one, you're crazy. Thought you had a Model A, did you?" He dropped the paper into his empty ashtray. "That stuff's confidential besides."

"Thanks for checking it out," Jack said.

"No problem," Vince said. "You boys take it easy now. I've got a date with a cinnamon roll." He waved to Julie as he drove off.

"Twelve forty-three," Jack said.

"What?"

"That's the street address for August Bartolozzi. Twelve forty-three Willner Street." He dashed to the pickup, grabbed a notebook, and scribbled down the numbers.

"And I always get blamed when we're late," Julie said.

"That's because it's always your fault," I said.

"Tell them it was a mudslide," Jack said. "They'll believe that."

I didn't get a chance to talk to Jack until we were home from school. He came by the house, and the two of us walked down toward the docks in the drizzling rain.

"Today was a bummer," I said. "I came in late to geography, so Crowell wouldn't let me take the quiz. And then he gave me a tardy slip besides."

"Did you tell him about the slide?"

"Yeah. He said my sad story was breaking his heart."

The lake was creeping up the boat ramp. The Batt brats were in the main parking lot, jumping into mud puddles. They stopped long enough to stick out their tongues and yell some dirty words.

"And Wendy was absent again," I went on. "She's got

strep throat. And I was all set to ask her to go to the basketball game."

"Your sad story is breaking my heart," Jack said. Halfway across the aluminum walkway he stopped and looked down into the muddy water. "August Bartolozzi. I wonder who he is."

"Or was," I said. "I should have known better than to listen to you. I spent half the night trying to figure out who around here could be a murderer. And now I find out it's probably some guy from San Francisco."

Jack shrugged. "I wouldn't rule out anything yet. I still think that was my old man."

"But it could be that August guy. Or Adolf Hitler. Or anybody else. The whole thing could have been an accident."

"Oh, sure. Somebody accidentally wired himself to the motor."

"That's not any crazier than the stuff you had me believing."

"Listen, Eddie, there's plenty we don't know, but I still think it was my father."

"Right. Your dad—murdered by one of the people around here. Talked to death by old Pooch maybe. Or stuffed with cinnamon rolls until he exploded. Or poisoned by Barbara Batt's health food." Jack started to say something, but I beat him to it. "I know. She wasn't even around here then. But you were. And you were a mean little devil nine years ago. Still are, for that matter. Maybe you did it."

Jack gave me a shove. "So make a joke out of it. But under my bed there's a bone that belonged to somebody. That's one thing you can't laugh off."

"Let's tell Vince," I said. "Let him figure it out."

"Oh, sure. And how do we explain not telling him before?"

"No problem. We don't mention the whole skeleton. We say we found this bone next to the motor. We didn't say anything at first because we thought he'd laugh at us for making a big deal out of nothing. Then he'll send the bone to some lab, and they'll find out it's human, and Vince can go on from there."

Jack stared at the water for a minute, then turned to me. "Listen, Eddie, you're right. We'll tell Vince. But first let's see what people around here remember about August Bartolozzi. Who knows? Maybe we can work out the whole thing ourselves."

"Jack Mason, boy detective," I said. "I can see it now. 'Excuse me, sir. Did you by any chance happen to kill August Bartolozzi?' "

Jack gave me a push. "Come on, Eddie. I've been thinking about this all day. We'll say we found something with his name on it."

"Like what?"

"A tackle box. How's that for simple and easy? We found a tackle box with his name on it, and we're wondering who he is. It'll work like a charm."

"Maybe." But I liked the idea. For years I had watched the reruns of *Columbo,* a show about a seedy detective who seems like a real dope. He's always bumping into furniture and spilling things and making dumb comments. But he's really a lot smarter than he seems. Being a kind of klutz myself, I liked a show where the dumb-acting clumsy guy ended up outsmarting everybody. And now I had a chance to be a real-life Columbo.

When Jack and I came across the walkway, Woody was winching the docks closer to shore. "Hey, detective," I muttered, "what are the next three words that will come out of Woody's mouth?"

"Who knows?"

"Try 'Not right now,' " I said, then called out, "Need some help, Woody?"

Woody kept cranking on the winch. "Not right now." I mouthed the words with him.

"How's that for deduction?" I said.

Jack pushed me aside. "Too easy."

With Woody busy, we began our detective work with Pooch. He was in the store, sitting on a stool and holding a ten-pound sack of sugar straight out in front of him. "You boys all ready to go for another swim?" he shouted.

"There's only one guy around here crazy enough to go swimming in January," I said.

"Some people can take it, and some can't. You two were about the sickest-looking pair I ever saw." He set the sugar on the counter and flexed his arms. "Only ten pounds, but after five minutes it gets a little heavy."

Jack didn't waste any time. "Hey, Pooch," he said, "did you ever hear of a guy named August Bartolozzi?"

When Columbo asks questions like that, people spill their coffee or snap pencils in two. All Pooch did was run his fingers through his hair. "I think so," he said. "August Barto—what?"

"Bartolozzi," Jack said, nodding to me.

"Yeah," Pooch said. "Yeah, I think so. He's an opera singer. I heard his name on one of the game shows."

That was all we got from Pooch.

When Woody came in for coffee, Jack tried the name on him.

"He got a boat here?" Woody asked.

"I don't think so. I just asked if you knew him."

Woody looked up from his coffee. "If he has a boat here, he'll be in the book."

"I don't think he has a boat here," Jack said, but he ended up getting out the notebook where Woody kept track of slip rentals. Sometimes it was easier to go along with Woody than to try to explain. There was no Bartolozzi in the book.

"Who said he had a boat here?" Woody asked.

"Nobody," Jack said. "I just wondered if you'd heard of him. We found a tackle box with his name on it. I thought maybe it was somebody you knew."

"If he'd had a boat here, his name would be in that book," Woody said.

I decided that was enough detective work for one afternoon. "I'd better get home and start on my algebra," I told Jack.

"Hey, Eddie, do me a favor," Pooch said, grabbing a 3 Musketeers bar off the shelf. "Take this up to Opal for me, will you? Tell her I said it was sweets for the sweet." He turned back to Woody. "You don't mind if I send your momma a little present, do you?"

"I don't care what you do," Woody said, heading for the door.

"Don't worry, Woodrow. If Opal and I get married, I'll be a good stepdaddy to you. I'll take you fishing and play baseball with you." He hooted when Woody slammed the door.

"Why don't you take this candy up there yourself?" I asked.

"Don't tell me how to handle women, Eddie, my boy. Besides, you owe me one. Didn't I go out in the pouring rain yesterday and get you some clothes? Didn't I help you out when you were sitting here shivering like a poodle with the mange?"

"I'll do it." I headed out the door before he got started again.

Jack walked up the hill with me. "Ask her if she's ever heard of August Bartolozzi. And ask your parents too."

I said I would, but the idea of playing Columbo had lost some of its thrill.

Ricky Batt was still jumping in puddles when we walked past. Tony had one of his shoes off and was using it to dip water out of a ditch.

"You want to come with me?" I asked Jack when we got to Woody's mailbox.

"You can handle it." He sounded a little down on detective work too.

Opal waved to me as I came up the driveway. As usual, she was sitting in her recliner beside the living room window. That way she could keep one eye on the television and the other on the road. She hardly ever left the house, but she knew plenty about what was happening around the marina.

She had been the cook at the restaurant until she'd had a massive heart attack. The doctors had said then that she didn't have much time left; but twelve years had gone by, and she was still around. Two of those doctors had died in the meantime.

"Come on in," she yelled before I could knock. I stepped inside and shut the door quickly, knowing that Opal hated drafts. The living room was as hot and muggy as a greenhouse.

Opal stayed in her recliner, an old quilt wrapped around her narrow shoulders and another one tucked up around her legs. She looked away from the talk show on the TV and said, "Good to see you, Eddie."

I handed her the candy bar. "Pooch says, 'Sweets for the sweet.'"

She ripped off the wrapper and laughed. "They're gonna haul that guy away one of these days. Crazier'n a wooden watch. Seventy-two years old, and he thinks he's a teenager." She waved the candy in my direction. "You want half?"

"No, thanks."

She took an enormous bite. "Did you see the TV my boy Franklin sent me for Christmas? He's working in the oil fields in Arabia, you know."

"Yeah." I had seen that TV half a dozen times in the past month, and I had almost memorized Franklin's life story. Whenever Opal got a telegram from him, we heard about it for weeks.

"I was just glad to get a TV that worked," Opal went on. "Our old one was shot. I never thought much about remote control. Always figured that anybody who was too lazy to get up and change the channel might just as well roll over and die. But you get used to it."

"I wish we had a remote control," I said.

"You don't need it," she snapped. "Young kid like

you, it won't hurt you to get up. You shouldn't be watching television anyway. There's so much dirt on, I'm surprised your mom lets you near the set. I saw something today that left me sitting here with my mouth open. I wouldn't dare tell you about it."

"Opal," I said when she took another bite of candy, "do you remember a guy around here named August Bartolozzi?"

She shook her head and kept chewing. (Nobody ever did that to Columbo.)

"We found a tackle box with his name on it. August Bartolozzi."

Opal kept shaking her head. "That's a terrible name. What kind of person would name a kid August? I can't imagine. I always thought a boy should have a name with a little class. But August? That's awful. Of course, Woodrow never did like his name. Called himself Woody right from the start. But Franklin wouldn't allow people to call him anything but Franklin until he got clear up into high school. Then it was Frank. He wasn't ever going to be called Frankie if he could help it."

"I don't blame him," I said. "I wouldn't be called Eddie if I had anything to say about it. You don't remember August Bartolozzi, huh?"

Opal shook her head and popped the last of the candy bar into her mouth. "Names matter. Don't let anybody tell you different. Somebody that calls himself Woody, you don't expect them to amount to much. Or what about a name like Pooch? But Franklin, that's another story."

It was a story I had heard more times than I cared to. I couldn't remember Franklin myself, but my dad said he was a whiner and a loafer. According to Opal, though, it was only a matter of time before he came back from Arabia and bought up the whole county. The first time she stopped for breath, I said, "Somebody's calling me," and headed for the door.

"Listen," she said, "you tell that crazy Pooch that he's wasting his money. I've had my fill of men. And if I wanted another one—which I do not—he sure ain't the one I'd pick."

At dinner that night, using my best Columbo style, I said, "Does anybody remember August Bartolozzi?"

Mom and Dad shook their heads.

Julie gasped and dropped her fork.

I turned and stared at her.

"Ken's here," she said, pointing out the window. "Tell him I'll be ready in just a minute."

I would have let the whole thing drop, but after dinner Mom checked her files. Nobody named Bartolozzi had ever stayed at the resort.

I got out my algebra, which went about as well as my detective work.

Later on, while Dad was watching a John Wayne movie and Mom was addressing brochures, Jack knocked on the door.

"Julie's not here," I told him.

"I know. I saw her go off with that turkey in his Firebird. She must be really bored." He never sounded jealous, and I couldn't tell if he was or not. "Let's go down to the docks."

I grabbed my raincoat and followed him out into the

dark. A strong south wind blew the rain into our faces. "What's going on?"

"I want to make a phone call."

"To Vince?"

"San Francisco Information. It's so obvious. I don't know why I didn't think of it earlier. How many guys named August Bartolozzi can there be in San Francisco? Or in the world, for that matter?"

"You're not going to call him, are you?"

"That'd be cute, wouldn't it, Eddie? Hello, Mr. Bartolozzi. We found a little something in Muir Lake that you left there."

"But what *are* you going to do?"

"First I'll get his number. Then we'll see."

But San Francisco Information had only three Bartolozzis listed—none of them named August. Jack took down all three numbers anyway.

"I knew it was too easy," I said.

"We're all right," Jack said. "Our man's bound to be related to one of these."

We put together a good story before we called those numbers: We had found a piece of jewelry with August's name engraved on it, and we were trying to return it. The story worked perfectly. Everybody Jack talked to was friendly and helpful. The only problem was that none of them had a relative named August.

On the third call Jack got hold of a woman who hadn't been married very long. She thought her husband had a cousin named August, and she went to check. "Now we're moving," Jack said.

Before the woman came back, the operator came on the line and asked for more money. Jack shoved in our last quarters, muttering, "Hurry up, lady." He held the receiver so that we both could hear.

"Sorry to take so long," the woman said. "My husband was down in the garage working on his car. He practically lives—"

"What did he say?" Jack asked her.

"His cousin is named Angelo."

"Not August?"

"No. Angelo," the woman said. "It was close, wasn't it?"

I stamped my foot and turned away. "If that isn't the—" I stopped short. Standing in the shadows, less than ten feet away, was old Pooch.

Jack banged down the receiver. "That—"

"Hi, Pooch," I called out to warn Jack.

Jack's head snapped around.

"What are you boys up to?" Pooch asked. His gray sweatshirt was soaked, so I knew he'd been standing there for a while.

"Not much," I said.

Pooch ran his fingers through his wet hair. "I guess you guys like standing in the rain while you talk on the phone."

"You bet," Jack said.

I headed for the walkway. "I still have some algebra to do. See you, Pooch."

"I'm about ready for a swim," he said. "You boys want to join me?"

Jack came after me. "That's okay."

Pooch let out a cackle. "Bunch of sissies around here."

Jack and I didn't talk until we were almost to my

driveway. Then I said, "Do you think he heard anything?"

"There wasn't much to hear."

"I hope he doesn't go telling everybody we were calling San Francisco." I looked over at Jack. "Does this stuff bother you? Do you get a little spooked sometimes?"

He laughed. "What's the matter, Eddie? You having bad dreams?"

"Not me. You can't have dreams if you don't sleep."

"Hey, it's not that bad."

"Why don't we tell Vince?" I said. "This detective stuff isn't working."

"Hold on a little longer. I want to try one more thing."

"What's that?"

"San Francisco. I'd like to stop by a place on Willner Street."

6

By morning Jack had a plan to get us to San Francisco. Every February there was a big boat show at the Cow Palace. The Los Cedros Chamber of Commerce always had a booth there with pictures of Muir Lake and brochures from all the resorts, including Grizzly Creek Marina. Jack figured we could use the show as an excuse to get away. Then we could do our detective work and still check out the new boats.

After school, while Julie did some shopping, Jack and I did a little more detective work at the town library. We went through all the phone books for the Bay Area and found four more Bartolozzis. We wasted several dollars calling them and finding out they'd never heard of August.

"San Francisco's our only chance," Jack said.

While the phone was handy, I also called Wendy and got her mother again. She said that Wendy had a sore throat and couldn't talk.

I wasn't about to quit that easily. "Can she listen?" I

asked. "I'll do the talking, and she can tap once for yes and twice for no." Mrs. Westfall laughed. "I'm serious. Can she do that?"

"Only for a minute. I'll get her."

The next thing I heard was a whispered "Hi."

"No talking," Mrs. Westfall called out.

"Hi, Wendy. Did your mom tell you the code? One tap for yes, two for no, three if you're being held prisoner against your will." Three quick taps from her. "That's what I figured. Well, you haven't missed much at school. Same old stuff. Somebody tried to assassinate Mr. Crowell, but he was wearing a bulletproof vest. And then when the cops came, they found marijuana growing in the teachers' lounge. But all the evidence was destroyed in the fire. I guess you heard that the whole junior class was trapped in the auditorium and got wiped out. All except for Delbert Markusson. He was out in the parking lot, sneaking a smoke. So Delbert's now junior class president. He's also vice-president and secretary. He says the junior prom may be canceled, or he may have it over at his house—if he can find a date."

"Wind it up," Mrs. Westfall said.

"Are you going to be back tomorrow?" Two taps. "How about Monday?" One loud tap. "I'm going to San Francisco this weekend. Shall I send you a postcard?" Tap. "I'll see you on Monday." She tapped, then hung up.

"Are you in love with Eddie Carter?" I said into the dead phone. I gave the receiver a loud slap.

I waited until dinner was over to talk to my parents about San Francisco. I had never been that far without one of them along, but I tried to keep the whole thing casual. "Jack's going to the boat show at the Cow Palace this Saturday," I said. "He says I can go along if I want."

"Doesn't he see enough boats around here?" Dad said.

"All the way to San Francisco?" Mom asked.

"It only takes about four hours," I said. "We'd leave early in the morning and come back that night."

"It's a long way," Mom said.

Dad stood up. It was time for the *CBS News.* "You sure you're going to the Cow Palace?"

That question caught me for a second. "Yeah."

Dad came out with a not-very-funny laugh. "There's plenty of mischief around here," he said. "I don't see much point in driving that far to look for it."

"We just want to go to the boat show. Jack wants to look at some jet skis and stuff like that."

Mom started to clear the table. "It's a long, long way."

"Don't worry," Julie said. "I'll go along and keep them out of trouble."

"Nobody invited you," I told her.

She gave me that cutesy look of hers that makes me want to vomit. "Not yet. But somebody might if I asked nicely."

"Why don't you stick to your own business?" I said.

Dad flipped on the TV and looked back at me. "What's the matter? You think Julie'd cramp your style?"

What could I say?

"I'm going to run over and ask Jack right now," Julie said. "I'd love to go to the boat show."

"Don't feel bad about horning in where you're not wanted," I called out.

She stopped in the doorway and looked back at me. "One question, Eddie. If Jack had his choice of somebody to take to San Francisco, which one of us do you think he'd take?"

"You make me sick."

"You'd better be nice to me," she said. "Otherwise we may not let you go along with us."

"Well," I said to Mom once Julie was gone, "can I go?"

"Let's see what happens."

"You mean you're waiting for Julie?"

"You bet," Dad said from the next room. "She'll keep you in line."

"When did I ever get out of line?"

Dad began to count on his fingers. "Let's see. There was the time you sneaked out the ski boat to impress that girl. And the time you hitchhiked into Los Cedros without telling anybody. And the time—"

"I'm sorry I asked," I said.

A few minutes later Julie came strolling back into the kitchen. "Guess what."

I borrowed a tactic from Ricky Batt and stuck out my tongue.

"Jack says he'd be glad to have me come along."

"Rotten, rotten, rotten," I said.

Mom smiled. "I'm sure you'll all have a good time."

On Saturday morning we left home a little after five o'clock. We drove for a couple of hours, then stopped for breakfast at a McDonald's. While we ate, Jack went ahead and told Julie about finding the bones and the license plate. He didn't mention anything about his father, though.

"Wow, this is spooky," Julie said. "You think maybe somebody around the marina could have been in on it?"

Jack shrugged. "Maybe. Maybe not. That's what we're trying to find out."

Julie looked at us and grinned. "This sounds like a lot more fun than a dumb boat show."

For the rest of the drive we listened to music from one of the San Francisco rock stations and made jokes about which one of us would be Sherlock Holmes and which one would play Watson.

When we got off the freeway and started working our way toward Willner Street, we shut off the radio. Julie had the map and was trying to navigate, but she didn't know about one-way streets. After a half hour of detours and dead ends, we finally turned onto Willner.

"Not exactly the high-rent district," Jack said.

Every block had several boarded-up buildings. All the fences and half the walls had been spray-painted with slogans, some in foreign languages.

"I wish I had a gun," I said.

Jack laughed. "Relax, Eddie. You sound like a hick from the sticks."

"I *am* a hick from the sticks. I just hope we don't get mugged."

He laughed again. "Who'd mug you? You don't have anything worth stealing."

"I'm putting my money in my shoe all the same."

The address we had was a three-story apartment

house. We parked the truck a half block down the street and walked back. I kept my eye on two little boys who were playing tag in the street. "I hope they leave the truck alone," I said.

"Settle down," Jack told me. "No kids in the world could be worse than the Batt brats."

Outside the door of the building were twelve mailboxes, some of them hanging open. Above the boxes were holes where doorbells had been. Snaky-looking wires hung out of some of the holes.

Only a few of the mailboxes had names on them. None of them said "Bartolozzi." "Now what?" I asked Jack.

"I guess we knock on some doors," he said.

The front door was locked, but we hung around the steps until an old man came out. Jack stepped past him and caught the door before it closed. "Excuse me, sir," he said. "Do you know a man named August Bartolozzi?"

The old man shook his head and went on down the steps.

The three of us went inside. The place smelled of mildew and stale cigarette smoke and other things I didn't try to guess. "We'll keep it simple," Jack said. "Just ask for August."

I stood back and let Jack knock on the first door. We heard somebody moving inside, but the door didn't open. Jack knocked again. Locks clicked, and the door opened a couple of inches. Two brass chains kept it from going any farther. A man in an undershirt looked out at us.

"We're looking for August Bartolozzi," Jack said.

"Wrong place." The door slammed.

"Maybe we'd better try a different technique," Jack said.

At the next door I knocked softly. When a gray-haired woman opened her door a crack, I launched into my story. "I'm sorry to bother you, ma'am, but I'm trying to locate my uncle. His name's August Bartolozzi."

"I don't know him," the woman said. "What's he look like?"

After swallowing once, I managed to say, "I'm not really sure."

The woman banged the door shut. "Don't know him."

Julie took the third one. "I hope you can help me," she told a black woman. "I'm trying to locate my father. His name is August Bartolozzi."

"He live here?" the woman asked.

"He used to. This is the last address we have for him."

"I don't know him, honey. I've only been here a couple of months. You better try some of the others. Maybe they can help you. Good luck now."

When we went to the fourth door, Julie knocked again. She seemed to be right for the job. She used the same story and got the same result. The man was friendly enough, but he couldn't help us.

We took the stairs to the next floor. Somebody had scribbled on the walls of the stairwell with a black crayon. The scribbler had a dirty mind but wasn't much of a speller.

"If they never heard of August," Jack told Julie, "ask them if they know anybody who's been around here a long time. We're talking about nine years maybe. Not many people would live here nine years—not if they could help it."

On that floor were an Oriental couple who didn't speak English and a brown-skinned man who said he'd only lived there a week. "And I'm moving as soon as I can find another place." Nobody answered the other two doors.

On the top floor we ran into a talker, a woman about fifty who smelled of wine. "I'm Lucille Rucker," she announced. She made us each tell her our names. She said she had been living in the building for three years. "I'm the old-timer. Started out on the first floor, then moved to this place. The stairs are hard, but it's lots quieter up here."

"You sure there's nobody that's been here longer?" Jack asked her.

"Course I'm sure. Most of these people are just fly-by-nighters. In one month, gone the next."

We thanked her but didn't get away until she told us about her daughter in Bakersfield who looked a little like Julie. "She has two kids. You wouldn't figure me for a grandmother, would you?"

She followed us down the hall to the next apartment. "No use bothering with those people. Young couple. Only been here a month or so. Not friendly at all."

Julie knocked on the door anyway. The man who answered said they had just moved there from Colorado and didn't know anybody.

"I told you," Lucille said.

"What about the others up here?" I asked her.

"Number twelve's not home," she said. "He works in

a liquor store down a couple of blocks. Opens up at six in the morning."

Jack got the man's name and the name of the store.

"And forget number eleven," Lucille said. "She's a dingbat."

"We'll try anyway," Julie said. She waved us on, then took Lucille's arm and walked her back toward her apartment.

I stepped up and knocked on number eleven. A woman opened the door immediately. She must have been standing there listening. "Yes?" she said through a tiny crack.

"Good morning," I said. "I'm trying to locate my father. He used to live here a long time ago."

"That's nice," the woman said.

"His name is August Bartolozzi."

She stared at me for a while, then said, "I don't know any Augusts. I knew a girl named May once, and there are lots of Junes around, but I never heard of anybody named August."

"Thanks, anyway," I said.

The woman opened the door wider. "Do you believe in reincarnation?" Jack and I backed away. "I've lived before. Many times."

"Right," Jack said, waving as we headed for the stairs.

Lucille was hanging on to Julie's arm. "You can't tell kids anything these days," she was saying. "I was her mother, but she wouldn't listen to a thing I said."

"I have to go," Julie said, prying her arm loose. "Thanks for your help."

"You might be better off not finding your daddy,"

Lucille called after us. "If he's the kind that ran off, maybe he'd just as well stay gone."

"We'd better check out that guy at the liquor store," Jack said as we clumped down the stairs. "Then maybe we'll try some of the other buildings around here."

"Really?" I said. "If the people here don't know him, what makes you think somebody next door would?"

Jack shrugged. "They probably won't. But I don't want to go home and start thinking of things we should have done. We'd better try everything."

"You know what?" I said. "This detective stuff could get old pretty fast."

We found the liquor store easily enough. It was a little hole in the wall with bars on the windows. We couldn't find a parking place, even after circling the block twice, so Jack parked in a bus zone while Julie and I went inside.

The place was empty except for a tall, thin man behind the counter. "What'll it be?" he asked before we were through the door.

"Are you Mr. Stouffer?" Julie asked.

He looked us over carefully. "Yeah."

"Somebody at your apartment house said we could find you here."

"That nosy Rucker bag, I'll bet. What do you want?"

Julie gave him the story about looking for her father. Mr. Stouffer was shaking his head before she had finished.

"I've only been there a year or so," he said. "Never heard of him."

I started for the door. "Well, thanks."

"Maybe you could help us," Julie said. "Is there anybody in that neighborhood who's been there a long time?"

"People come and go," he said. "Except old Rucker. She's been there forever, I think."

When Julie and I went back outside, the pickup was gone. We stood on the curb and waited. Everybody who came past looked like a criminal. I tried to look casual while thoughts about kidnappers and slashers flashed through my mind.

When I spotted Jack's truck, I shouted, "Here he comes!"

"You really are a hick," Julie said, but she looked relieved too.

"I had to move," Jack told us. "A bus was coming. You weren't worried, were you?"

"Not me," I said. "I like being surrounded by killers and dope fiends."

"You two find out anything?"

"No," I said. "Same old story."

Jack looked over at us. "I've been thinking. Somebody owns that place. And the owner would know who lived there."

"I'll go back and ask," I said, pushing open the door. "If you have to circle the block, make it fast."

Stouffer was in the same spot behind the cash register.

"Could you tell me who owns your building?" I asked him.

"No idea." He reached into his pocket for a cigarette.

"Then who do you pay your rent to?"

Stouffer lit his cigarette before answering. "Guy named Felix. He's sort of the manager, I guess. Rents the places, picks up the money, says he'll fix something and never does."

"Where would we find him?"

"I don't know. He doesn't live there, that's for sure."

An old man stepped inside and bought a cigar, paying for it with a nickel and a wad of pennies. When he left, I asked, "This Felix, do you have his phone number?"

Stouffer smiled for the first time. "You want to see Felix, huh? There's a vacancy sign back at the building. Just call the number on that and tell Felix you're thinking about a one-year lease. He'll be over in a hurry."

Jack was still in the bus zone when I came out. We drove back to the apartment house and hunted for the vacancy sign.

We found some tape on the window of the front door, but no sign. We checked the street then and found the sign—ripped into four pieces—underneath a parked car.

Jack carried the sign back to his pickup. "We've got to be careful," he said. "This is the only chance we have. Do we get him here, or do we try it over the phone?"

"Get him here," Julie said.

"But if he comes here thinking he's going to rent the place, what's he going to say when we start asking questions?"

Julie smiled. "I think we can handle it."

We had to drive a long way before we found a phone booth with a phone that worked. After Julie made the call, we got some hamburgers at a Burger King and went back to wait for Felix.

Felix left his pickup double-parked and marched toward us. He was a small dark man in paint-stained coveralls. His hair was slicked back, and he had a thick mustache that curled up at the ends. He looked over the three of us and asked, "Who's the apartment for?"

"Jack and I," Julie said in a little-girl voice. She grabbed Jack's arm and giggled.

"You got any money?"

Julie nodded. "It's okay if it's in cash, isn't it? We don't have a bank account set up yet."

Felix headed for the steps. "I'll show you the place."

We went up one flight of stairs, and Felix opened number eight, which was just one big room with a tiny bathroom behind a curtain. The place smelled of smoke and sour milk. The walls were painted a pale yellow that didn't quite cover the flowered wallpaper underneath. Felix opened a closet and pulled down a bed. "Ever see one of these?" he asked.

"Wow," Julie gurgled.

Felix slapped the mattress. "It's a Murphy bed."

"That's so neat," Julie said.

"What do you say?" Felix asked while he pushed the bed back up and shut the doors. "You want it or not?"

Julie squeezed Jack's arm and said, "Honey, what do you think?"

"It's kind of small," he said.

"For that money you don't get a penthouse," Felix said.

"This is really lucky," Julie told Felix. "We just happened to see the sign. We were driving by because my uncle used to live here awhile back. Maybe in this very apartment. I can't remember for sure."

Felix shifted his weight from one foot to the other. "Make up your minds, kids."

"Do you remember August Bartolozzi?" Julie asked him. "He lived here a long time ago."

For the first time since we started, I saw a Columbo-style reaction. Felix stepped back, his eyes narrowing. "What about him?"

"You remember him then?" Julie said.

Felix shrugged. "Sort of."

"Maybe you could tell us about him. We lost track of him."

Felix studied her for a minute. "He only lived here a little while. Who knows? Maybe ten years ago."

"But you remember him?" Julie went on in that air-head voice of hers. "What an amazing memory you have!"

Felix took a step toward the door. "If you're looking for his stuff or anything, forget it. It's long gone."

"Oh, no," Julie bubbled. "We're not interested in anything like that. We just wondered what happened to him."

Felix looked at each of us. "You never heard about that?"

"About what?" Julie asked.

"He got himself shot," Felix said.

We all stared at him.

Felix looked away and laughed. "What can I say? He stuck up a bank and got shot. That's why I remember the name. I mean, how many of your renters do that? Nobody claimed his stuff, so I just sold it for the rent. That's the way it goes."

"When was this?" Jack asked him.

"Who knows? Long time back. You kids want this place or not?"

"I'm not sure," Julie said. "Do you remember anything about Uncle August? What he was like or anything?"

"Sorry," Felix said. "He was just a renter. He got himself shot, and I ended up with his TV, a little black-and-white job. It still works, believe it or not. I keep it out in my shop."

"We'll think about the place," Jack said. "We'd like something a little cheaper."

Felix shook his head. "Anything cheaper, and you'll end up living with rats. This ain't a mansion, but there's no rats. And the heat works."

"We'll think about it," Jack told him.

"Then think about it outside." Felix headed for the hall. "I got things to do. You want the place today, call me. By tomorrow it'll be gone." He led the way downstairs and walked straight to his double-parked pickup without ever looking back at us. He pulled open the pickup door and turned to Julie. "Last chance."

"We'll think about it," she said.

Felix climbed into the truck and drove away.

"Let's go to the boat show, Sherlock," Jack said to Julie. "We've earned it."

By the time we found the Cow Palace, it was late afternoon. I rushed around and grabbed every brochure I could find, to prove we'd been there. I looked at some bass boats and jet skis, but nothing interested me much.

I just wanted to go home. But the home where I wanted to go—where everything was safe and sure—didn't exist anymore.

7

The next morning Mom dragged Julie and me out of bed so that the four of us could have a leisurely breakfast together. Dad, who had just finished his Sunday morning ten-mile run, was the only one at the table who didn't look exhausted.

Once she'd had some coffee, Mom wanted to know all about the boat show. I hauled out the brochures and tried to remember something I'd seen. All I could think about was that apartment house and the way it had smelled.

"Did you keep the boys out of trouble, Julie?" Dad asked.

"What can you do with Eddie? He was chasing girls all over the place. He's not even fussy. Anybody between ten and twenty-five. He kept sliding up next to them and talking about his place on the lake."

"Public relations," I said.

Dad grinned at me. "Did you go straight to the boat show, or did you stop somewhere else?"

I didn't have an answer for that, but Julie sailed right in. "Are you kidding? That would be too easy. We had to drive around a little, get lost a few times, drive the wrong way up one-way streets."

"Was it worth the trip?" Mom asked.

"Yeah," I said. "It was interesting." I must have said that wrong. Dad didn't ask any more questions, but he watched me all through breakfast.

On Monday morning I spotted Wendy outside the algebra classroom. To judge by the way she looked, strep throat must have agreed with her.

Wayne Parks was standing beside her. He gave me a dirty look when I came up and said, "Good to see you back."

Wendy smiled at me. "Hi, Eddie."

I looked at Wayne. "You really think she'll do it?"

"What are you talking about?"

"You know. Tina Fisher and her bet."

"What's going on?" Wendy asked.

"Oh," I said, "Tina's supposed to go skinny-dipping in the pool. There's about a hundred dollars riding on it."

Wayne's eyes bugged out. "When?"

"Right now, I think. A bunch of seniors were standing around out there when I came by."

"Yeah, sure," Wayne said, but he took off down the hall.

Wendy looked at me. "Skinny-dipping?"

"The walk'll be good for him," I said. "Here's your postcard." I had forgotten to buy one in San Francisco, so I gave her one of Grizzly Creek Marina.

Wendy looked at it and laughed. "You got this in San Francisco?"

"No, but I liked it better than the ones I saw down there. Who needs an orange bridge anyway?"

She slipped the card into her algebra book. "Thank you."

People were standing all around us, but I didn't want to pass up the chance. I moved up close to her and said, "You want to go to the basketball game with me on Friday?"

"I can't," she said. "My parents won't let me go out." She motioned for me to follow her, then took a few steps down the hall. "Would it be too much like sixth grade if I met you there?"

That was what I'd had in mind when I asked her, but I didn't let on. "No problem," I said.

As soon as school was over, Jack, Julie, and I headed for the town library, which had the *San Francisco Chronicle* on microfilm. Julie had used the microfilm reader for history papers, so she knew what we were in for. "We'll just do the first section," she said. "Then we'll zip through the sports and the want ads."

After we had spent half an hour on the first week of January, Jack figured we had to change our tactics. "We could be here a month. A bank robbery's not that big a deal in San Francisco, but if the guy was shot, the story should be on the first three pages."

By the five o'clock closing time I had microfilm elbow from turning the crank and a headache from looking at all those spinning words. We had made it through May without seeing the name Bartolozzi, and I had read about enough robberies to convince me never to go back to San Francisco.

"Tomorrow," Jack said. "We'll find it tomorrow."

The next afternoon we skipped over to September. "We can always go back," Jack said. "But there are too many people around the lake in the summertime. You wouldn't dare dump a body then."

"Right," I said. "I dump all my bodies in the fall."

We got even faster with the microfilm reader, each of us skimming the stories on one section of the page. I thought we were getting good at it, but we missed the main story.

We were starting November when I saw a boxed piece headed GRISLY FIND IN RICHMOND DISTRICT GARAGE. I stopped cranking and examined a picture of a woman pointing to a garage door, then one of police carrying a covered stretcher. I skimmed down the page as the woman told of finding a body in the garage she had rented to a "nice enough young man." Then I let out a yelp that brought a warning look from the librarian. "Police have tentatively identified the dead man as August Bartolozzi, 24, a suspect in the October 27 robbery of the Richmond office of the Bank of . . ."

We backed up five days and found a short article on the bottom of the first page. (I don't know how we missed it the first time through.) It said that the bank had been robbed by two white males wearing nylon stocking masks. An off-duty policeman had spotted them running from the bank. Several shots had been exchanged before the suspects had escaped in a green

Plymouth sedan. The policeman, who had fired four shots, said he believed both suspects were seriously wounded. The Plymouth had been found parked in a driveway a few blocks away, the seat covered with blood.

"Now we're getting somewhere," I blurted out before I noticed the odd look on Jack's face.

We combed the next days' papers page by page, but there were no more stories until the garage piece. After that we found an article with the headline ROBBERY SUSPECT POSITIVELY IDENTIFIED, which said that a bullet removed from Bartolozzi's body matched that from the policeman's revolver. The car in the garage was registered to Bartolozzi, but the license plates were missing. The investigation was continuing.

Jack gave me a shove and grinned. "Beautiful," he muttered.

"What are you talking about?" Julie whispered.

"Things are looking good," Jack said.

The following day's paper contained an article called ROBBER'S SHADOWY BACKGROUND. The reporter had talked to several people living at the apartment house on Willner Street. All of them said Bartolozzi was unfriendly. "He wouldn't even look at you," one woman said. Bartolozzi had served in the army and received a general discharge. He had recently moved to San Francisco, where he had worked as a dishwasher and a parking attendant. Army records showed he had originally come from Cleveland, but no family could be located there.

The article finished with a statement from a man who had worked with Bartolozzi in a parking garage:

"He seemed to think he was better than the rest of us. I told him one time that the boss would fire him if he didn't move a little faster, and he said he didn't care, his future didn't depend on parking cars."

That line sent chills up my back.

We searched through the next three weeks of the paper without finding any more stories. Then we went back and reread the stories we had. I started to scribble some notes, but Jack said, "Don't bother, Eddie. We're all finished."

We replaced the rolls of microfilm and headed for the door. Jack shoved open the door and leaped down the steps. "Hey-hey," he yelled.

"What's going on?" Julie asked him.

"I feel great," he shouted.

Julie turned to me. "Do you know what's gotten into him?"

"Not really."

Jack came trotting up to her. "You know that guy we found in the lake? That was my old man."

"What?" Julie said. "How do you know?"

"Has to be."

She took a step back. "And that's why you're jumping up and down?"

"No. I thought he'd been murdered, see? And I was afraid my mom had done it. That's why I couldn't tell the sheriff. Now I find out what really happened, and it's a whole lot better than I thought." He jogged toward the truck, slapping each parking meter as he passed it.

Julie grabbed my arm. "Eddie, have I missed something?"

"I don't think so."

"Then Jack's just guessing, right?"

"Kind of. His father disappeared back then, so it sort of fits, I guess."

Jack stopped by the pickup and opened the door on the passenger side. "Hop in, and I'll tell you the whole story."

Julie stepped in and slid across the seat. "Is this true, or are you guessing?"

"Yes and yes." Jack trotted around the front of the truck and pulled open the other door. "I'm guessing, but it's all true." He climbed in and started the engine.

"Let's hear it," Julie said.

Jack pulled away from the curb. "Okay, the first thing you have to realize is that my old man was a born loser. He was also a lowlife and a creep, but that's beside the point. He was a loser. No matter what he tried, he messed it up. My mother had a restaurant when they got married, but the old man gambled it away. He always had some big deal going, but nothing ever worked out.

"So it's a perfect ending for a loser. He and August Bartolozzi—who sounds like another loser—try to knock over a little neighborhood bank. They have their big hotshot plan: They'll ditch their getaway car, hop in August's car, and hide in the rented garage until things are quiet. But an off-duty cop happens to be standing there on the sidewalk, and they get shot. Typical brilliant John Mason plan with its typical ending."

"I'm glad you think it's funny," Julie said. "That makes one of you."

"So August dies," Jack went on, "and my old man is

shot. What would he do? He'd do what he always did when he was in trouble. He'd run to Mom for help. But he died, and Mom was stuck with a problem. If she called the cops, then I'd find out my daddy was a crook, and kids at school would give me a rough time. So she saved all kinds of trouble—and funeral expenses, too—by dumping him in the lake. It was a smart move. Nobody found out, and we didn't have to move away or anything. It all worked out for the best."

"And what proof do you have for this?" Julie asked him.

"Not a speck. But it had to be that way."

"Wonderful!" She turned in my direction. "It's typical Jack. He tries to be so cool and logical, then jumps to ridiculous conclusions."

Jack laughed. "Typical Julie. If she doesn't like the answer, she figures you've done the problem wrong."

"You don't *know* anything," she said.

"I know one thing. I haven't felt this good for a week." He reached over and flipped on the radio.

A few minutes later Julie said, "Maybe nobody from the marina's involved at all."

"Maybe I can fly, too," Jack said.

"And there's no reason to think that's your father, except that he went away about that time."

"That's a pretty big except."

"But you could be wrong."

"Look," Jack said, "we know the guy in the lake is tied up with the robbery, right? The license plate shows that."

"Okay, but—"

"Now," he went on, "why would a wounded bank

robber come down Grizzly Creek Road to the marina unless he knew somebody there?"

"He could have been looking for a hideout."

Jack laughed. "Who dumped him in the lake then?"

"Maybe there were two people," Julie said. "One of them had been shot, and the other was looking for a good place to get rid of the body."

Just then we drove onto the bridge that crosses the east arm of Muir Lake. Jack didn't say anything until we were almost in the center of the bridge. Then he pulled to the side and stopped. "Tell me something," he said. "If you wanted to get rid of a body, why not do it here? Two hundred feet of murky water right below you. Why go all the way down to the marina and get a boat?" He laughed and shoved down on the gas pedal.

"I haven't had as long to think about it as you have," Julie said. "But that doesn't make you right."

Jack laughed at her, and she moved so far away from him that she had me squashed against the door.

"Don't take it out on me," I said.

"I just need some time to think about it," she said.

"Take all the time you want," Jack told her. "I already told you what happened."

"You make me so mad," she shouted. "You're so stupid sure of yourself, and it's nothing but a bunch of crazy guesses."

Jack grinned. "Prove me wrong then."

8

When we got home that afternoon, we found a note from Mom with instructions for dinner. "You do the cooking," Julie said, heading into Mom's office. "I want to check the old records while Mom's not here."

I followed her as far as the door. "What are you looking for? Think we might have had a bank robbers' convention scheduled that weekend?"

"I want to see who was around, that's all. I think somebody ought to try working with facts."

"Jack could be right, you know," I said.

She opened a file drawer. "If he is, it's pure luck. He's so bullheaded. 'Prove me wrong then.' I'd love to wipe that smug look off his face."

I had the spaghetti sauce simmering and was putting the final touches on a salad when she called out, "Finally."

"What'd you find?"

"It's the datebook for that year."

Until Mom started working with a computer two

years ago, she had kept all the reservations in oversize datebooks.

I gave Julie a couple of minutes, then asked, "Anybody staying here then?"

"I guess not. The twenty-seventh was a Friday, though, and we had a wedding reception at the Pelican's Perch on Saturday. Somebody was probably here decorating on Friday night."

"And after they strung crepe paper, they dumped the body, right?"

"Here's something funny. A little note for the twenty-fifth. 'Roy S.F. Twelve: thirty-five.' You know what that means?"

"Yeah, Dad was in San Francisco. Unless you figure it's Super Fly. Or State Farm. Hey, I know, it's what I'm making right now. S.F.—Spaghetti Fantastic."

"And here's a note on the following Tuesday. 'Roy back.' That means he was in San Francisco the whole week."

I set a pan of water on the stove. "Julie, somehow I can't picture Dad as a bank robber. He'd figure it was too much bother."

"No argument there," she said. "But at least we know something Jack doesn't."

I spotted Mom coming up the driveway. Julie managed to get things put back and to make it to the kitchen in time. The only disaster that night was the spaghetti sauce, which I managed to burn. And Julie was rotten enough to whisper, "S.F.—Spaghetti Forgettable."

Things were quiet on the way to school the next morning. Another storm had blown in during the night, but the chill in the pickup had nothing to do with the outside weather. Julie kept her eyes glued on the windshield and her lips pressed together. Jack grinned and hummed along with the radio.

About a mile from school Julie flipped off the radio and announced, "My father was in San Francisco when that bank was robbed."

"Don't worry," Jack said. "He didn't have anything to do with it."

"He wouldn't have to be a bank robber," I said. "What if Dad's car was parked somewhere and the robber crawled into the back seat and Dad didn't look back there until he was home and then—"

"You've been watching too much television," Jack said.

"Okay," Julie told him, "I can't buy Eddie's story either, but there are lots of other possibilities."

Jack laughed. "Including the possibility that I'm right."

Julie moved away from him, squashing me against the door again. "Go ahead and be that way. Eddie and I are going to keep looking for some facts."

Jack shrugged. "That's okay. You two Sherlocks keep at it. I don't mind being proved right."

For all I knew, Jack could have been right. But I wanted proof. I wanted to find out exactly what had happened, down to the last detail. Until I did, I was never going to be completely comfortable. I would be looking at people I'd known all my life and wondering about them. And that's no way to live.

In my geography class I thought about bank robberies while Mr. Crowell talked about the early days of Los Cedros. Then he assigned a five-page paper on some aspect of local history. I was still in my first-period fog and didn't react until Eric Jurgenson asked if he could do a history of his father's creamery. "Perfect," Mr. Crowell said.

My hand shot up. "Can I do Grizzly Creek Marina?"

When he nodded, I felt everything fall into place. That project would be a perfect cover for my detective work. I had an excuse to ask all the questions I wanted.

Mom was really excited about my project. "I've been meaning to do a history for years," she said. "I've been saving things, but somehow I never get around to putting them all together."

She brought out shoeboxes full of pictures and old brochures. She even had lists of famous people (ballplayers and actors) who had been there. Five pages would be a snap.

I already knew some of the marina's history. Just after I was born, my grandfather had traded some timberland for the marina and offered Mom a partnership. The place was falling to pieces then, but he and Mom loved the lake and loved the idea of living there.

Dad was against the whole thing. He had a good, steady job at the lumberyard, and he figured one job was all anybody needed. He finally agreed to the move with the understanding that the marina and its problems belonged to Mom and Grandpa.

Dad was still holding to that agreement. Except for fixing up our house, he never lifted a finger around there, even in the busy summers when the rest of us were putting in twelve-hour days.

After Grandpa had died, Dad tried to get Mom to sell the place. Things were pretty slow then, and Dad figured Mom was spending all her time without getting much in return. But Mom wouldn't listen. The resort was home, and she wasn't about to give it up.

After looking through the shoeboxes for half an hour, I dug out the datebook I wanted. I turned to October, then carried the book into the kitchen. "Mom, I was checking a date and came across this. What does 'Roy S.F. Twelve thirty-five' mean?"

She studied the page for a minute. "I guess your dad was in San Francisco for something."

"I'll ask him when he comes." I started back to the office.

"Wait a minute," Mom said. "Bring me that." She looked at the datebook again, flipped a page, and started to laugh. "Whatever you do, don't ask your father about that one."

"Why not?"

"We fought about that for five years. I'll bet we could get going on it again if we tried."

"Really?"

Mom handed me the datebook. "Don't you remember the time you went to San Diego to visit Grandma Carter?"

"But this says S.F."

"You drove to San Francisco and took the plane."

Then I remembered it—a little. It was my first ride in an airplane. And Julie and I had gone to the San Diego Zoo, where I had seen a giant tortoise. "Yeah," I said. "I had to tell my kindergarten class all about it. But what was the problem?"

"I couldn't go. We had a huge wedding reception scheduled for that Saturday, and I had to be here. Grandma Carter was sick, and your father thought I should go."

"You fought for five years about that?"

Mom laughed. "Not continuously."

Later on I got Julie aside and told her. "There you go. Real facts. Dad's innocent, and you and I have alibis."

"Keep digging," she said.

That evening I walked down to the docks to call Wendy. I hadn't had a real chance to talk to her since Monday. With our crazy class schedules the only time I saw her was before and after algebra, and Wayne Parks was always hanging around.

Wendy's phone rang once, and an answering machine clicked on. A man's voice said, "The number you have reached is five-five-five-three-eight-four-one. If you would like to leave a message, please do so after you hear the bell." I hung up and listened to the telephone swallow my money.

I came back an hour later, bringing my mother's kitchen timer with me. When I got the answering machine again, I waited for the bell, then held my nose and said, "The number you have reached is five-five-five-nine-eight-nine-two. Please leave a message after you hear the bell." I rang the bell on the timer and hung up. Let them figure out that one.

(If they were curious enough to call the number,

they'd get a dial-a-prayer deal from one of the churches.)

The next day Jack wanted to know what fascinating discoveries we had made. We didn't say a thing. I wasn't about to tell him we had eliminated Dad. "What's the matter?" he asked. "Detective business a little slow?"

Because of that, Julie volunteered to help me go through the shoeboxes. We started by sitting on the floor with a box apiece and plowing through. We didn't know what we were looking for, but I hoped something might jump out at us.

It didn't.

I finally began sorting by dates—early pictures to the far left, recent ones to the right. Any picture taken within a year of the bank robbery went into a special stack by my right knee.

The early pictures showed how crummy things had been when Mom and Grandpa started. The docks were tiny, and the cabins were unpainted shacks. Then, as the years went by, buildings got painted, and dirt paths got paved. But the place still looked a little seedy.

I ended up with seven pictures in my special pile, none of them very exciting. The top one was of Pooch sitting in a white rowboat and holding up a string of fish.

"He hasn't changed much," I said.

Julie held the picture out to Mom, who was shaking her head at the mess on her office floor. "Are you sure that date is right? It could have been taken yesterday."

Mom glanced at it and smiled. "Pooch hasn't changed in the whole time I've known him. That's the old boat he used to haul out of the water every night. He was too cheap to rent a slip for it."

"Why didn't he keep it with his houseboat?" I asked.

"He didn't have a houseboat in those days. He lived in a little trailer up past the Masons' place. He already lived there when we bought the marina. He sort of came with the property."

I looked up from my pile of pictures. "When'd he get the houseboat?"

"Later on. I don't know when. He inherited some money and bought that houseboat and turned into our best customer. Up until then he was a pest. Always scrounging for something free. He was pretty hard up, I guess."

Julie and I glanced at each other. Here was something else Jack didn't know.

Mom knelt beside me and flipped through some of the early pictures. The ones of Grandpa got to me. I started remembering all the horsey rides and the stories about sea captains and the toys he whittled. My throat got tight, and I had to go to the kitchen for a drink of water.

As soon as Mom left, I went back to the special pile. The last picture was of the restaurant kitchen. Jack's mother and some other people dressed in white were standing beside a ratty-looking stove. Julie, also in white, was kneeling in front of the others.

"Boy, the kitchen looks different," I said to her. "Who's the funny-looking kid in the front row?"

Julie leaned back and studied the picture. "I remember when this was taken. That's probably the best kitchen crew this resort ever had. I worked like a trooper."

"Nine years ago? You were only eight years old. What is this—child labor?"

"I thought it was fun. I ran my legs off, did more than any busperson we've had since. I used to get fifteen percent of the tips instead of the usual ten because I worked so hard." She handed me the picture. "You recognize the girl standing next to Louise? The blond one?"

I looked at the picture again. "No. Who is it?"

"Barbara Batt."

I took another look. "Barbara? A blonde?"

"They had peroxide in those days too. She had just graduated from high school, and I thought she was the greatest thing going. She was always fixing my hair and teaching me new dances."

I took the picture into the kitchen. "I didn't know Barbara Batt worked here," I said to Mom.

"She was just here one summer." Mom glanced at the picture and handed it back. "Poor kid, her mother was remarrying, and she didn't have anyplace to go. I said she could work here."

"How'd she do?"

Mom shrugged. "She was fine in the restaurant. She worked hard, and the customers liked her."

"But there was a problem, right? I can hear it in your voice."

"Your dad and I weren't ready for a teenager just then. I sort of felt responsible for her, I guess."

I looked down at the picture. "What about Roger? Did he ever work here?"

Mom smiled. "I'm not sure Roger ever worked anywhere. He hung around here that summer, though. He was a lot older than Barbara. At least it seemed like it then. And we weren't sure she ought to be around him."

"I get the picture."

Mom laughed. "We were young ourselves. We didn't know how to handle a girl that age."

"Why? What happened? Did you have a lot of trouble?"

Mom began searching in the cupboard for something. "Oh, I don't want to go into it. We were worried about her, and she was at the age where she didn't want any advice."

I decided it would be easier to get the story from Opal. "I have to see Jack for a minute," I said, heading for the door.

"Hurry back," Mom called after me. "I want that office cleaned up before dinner."

Getting an answer from Opal wasn't all that easy, though. Before I was through the door, she started in about something she'd seen on *General Hospital.* A nurse on the program had given an overdose to somebody. "That finished me," Opal said. "I decided right here and now I'm never going to a hospital again. I'll die here first."

Once that was taken care of, I told her that I was doing a history of the marina. That got her going again. "You can put me in your history," she said. "Me and Woody. I was the best cook this place ever had, and Woody's the biggest sucker around."

I tried to ask about Barbara, but Opal wasn't finished.

"Woody never should have come here. Your grandpa and Woody were supposed to be partners, but Woody just ended up a hired hand."

"I didn't know that," I said, although I'd heard it from her before.

"I don't blame your grandpa. It's Woody's fault. He didn't stand up for himself. No ambition—that's his problem. No get-up-and-go. You look at this house here. You see how awful it is?"

I looked around, wondering what she didn't like.

"It's worth your life to try to get Woody to do anything with this place. He's out there every morning, opening that store and puttering around with his boats, but do you think he has a few minutes to fix something around here? Not on your life."

"Come on, Opal," I said. "This place looks pretty good."

"I used to take care of things, but I can't get around much now. When we first came here, Franklin used to help, but then he went off to the army. If he lived around here, this place would be a whole lot different, let me tell you."

"I just found out that Barbara Batt worked here as a waitress," I broke in. "Do you remember that?"

"Nothing wrong with my mind, Eddie. My body's all broke down, but my memory's all right. That girl was nothing but trouble. About drove your mom and your grandpa crazy. She was always zipping off with that guy on his motorcycle. What's his name? The one she's married to?"

"Roger."

"Trash. He always was. Worthless as they come. But

you couldn't tell her that. Young ones like her, they won't listen. That Roger almost killed me."

"He did?" This was *real* news.

"I was almost dead that summer. Had another bad heart attack. Doctors didn't give me no chance at all. And it seems like every time I'd get to sleep, that hoodlum would go tearing by on his motorcycle and wake me up. It's a wonder I didn't die."

"Oh." I tried not to sound too disappointed.

"Your grandpa hated him. Everybody did. They would have run him off, but that girl said if Roger left, she was going too. I would have said good riddance to both of 'em, but your mom was trying to help the girl."

"That's Mom," I said.

"Girl wasn't worth it, though. She had her chances. When she first came here, Franklin was sort of interested in her. He was out of the army by then. I was hoping he'd get a girl and settle down. But he wasn't her type. She liked trash. So pretty soon he went off and ended up going to Arabia." Opal pointed a finger at my chest. "You know, Eddie, when I see that girl and those raggedy kids, I figure she got just what she deserves. Things could have been real different for her."

"Somebody's calling me," I said.

"I don't understand your mother," Opal went on. "That girl took off without even saying good-bye. Just up and left one night. And your mom never heard a word from her for years and years. Then she showed up here last fall, and your mom took her in again."

I stopped in the doorway. "When did she leave? Barbara, I mean."

Opal shook her head. "I don't know. In the fall sometime." She picked up the remote control box. "Did I show you the TV my boy Franklin sent me for Christmas?"

The channels were still flipping when I closed the door.

9

After talking to Opal, I headed for Jack's place. I planned to show Jack the picture of Barbara, tell him that both she and Roger had been here nine years ago, then take off. That would give him something to think about.

But nobody was home. I checked the garage, saw that the pickup was gone, and started back. Before I got to the end of the driveway, Jack's mother turned in. She stopped her old VW beside me and rolled down the window. "How you doing, Eddie?"

"Hi, Louise. I was just looking for Jack."

"I met him on the road just now. He finally got around to hauling some of those old car parts back to the wrecking yard. I just hope he doesn't trade for something else."

"Maybe I'll catch him later on."

"He may not be home too early. He's having dinner with Lisa or Linda—I forget which."

"I'll see him tomorrow," I said. "How are things at

the junior high?" She worked as a cafeteria cook during the school year.

"Noisy as ever."

"I've got a picture to show you." I handed her the snapshot of the kitchen crew.

She looked at it and chuckled. "That was a long time ago. Look at Julie. Of course I haven't changed any." She handed it back. "Where'd you dig that up?"

"Mom had it. I'm doing a history of the marina for my geography class."

"That's quite a project."

"Yeah. It's tough keeping the time straight. When did you come here?"

"I've been here twelve years, believe it or not. Opal was in the hospital, and your mom had already fired two cooks. I said I'd try it for a week, and I've been here ever since." She looked at me. "Am I going to be in your report?"

"You bet. Mom says your cooking turned this place around."

She laughed. "Tell those junior high turkeys that."

I showed her the picture again. "Do you remember when this was taken?"

"Not really."

"Julie says the girl next to you is Barbara Batt."

Louise brought the picture up close to her glasses. "That's her, all right. I didn't recognize her."

"I guess she caused a few problems that summer."

"Kept things interesting," Louise said. "Your grandpa was fit to be tied. Nobody had any use for that Roger except Barbara. Greasy-haired hoodlum on a motorcycle. But he was her Prince Charming, I guess. Nobody could tell her a thing." She handed me the picture. "I should talk. I wouldn't listen to anybody either, and I was a lot older than Barbara. And my Prince Charming was the biggest frog of all."

The opportunity was too good to pass up. "I've been trying to remember. When did Mr. Mason leave here?"

"Not soon enough. Listen, Eddie, he doesn't belong in your history. He never did stay here much. Just stopped off once in a while to raise a little fuss. About the time I filed for divorce, he disappeared for good. Wasn't about to pay child support."

"Do you know where he is now?"

She shook her head. "No idea, thank goodness."

"He doesn't write to Jack or anything?"

"That's not his way. He likes the big show." She shifted into first gear, then looked up at me with a twisted smile. "He'll probably show up for Jack's high school graduation and buy him a new car and play the long-lost daddy. That's the way he operates."

I knew right then that Jack was wrong about his mother. She really believed that Jack's father was still alive.

I sprinted back to my house. I was more confused than ever, but I felt pretty good. Just like Columbo, I had kept asking innocent questions until I had made an important discovery. I couldn't wait to tell somebody, and Julie was my only candidate.

"Don't worry," I told Mom as I banged the front door closed. "I'll clean things up right away."

"No hurry, unless you start getting hungry," she said. "You don't eat until that mess is taken care of."

I rushed into the office. Julie was still on the floor,

surrounded by stacks of pictures. "Julie," I whispered, "I just found out something. Jack's all wrong. His mother's not involved."

"Big deal," Julie said. "I already knew that. Jack's being utterly ridiculous." She shoved a pile of pictures toward me. "And I don't appreciate your running off and leaving me to do the dirty work."

Columbo didn't have a sister—I'm sure of that.

After dinner that night I got a flashlight and headed over to the Batts' cabin with the picture of the kitchen crew. I didn't have a real plan. I figured I could show Barbara the picture, talk about my report, and see where things went. After my discovery that afternoon, I had more faith in Columbo's methods than before.

The cabins were scattered in the pines behind the restaurant, connected to the lower parking lot by gravel trails. Our brochure called the cabins "rustic," which meant wooden floors and open rafters. Our place wasn't exactly the Holiday Inn, but when the lake was full, we didn't have many vacancies.

Since the cabins had no heating, nobody had ever stayed there in the winter before. In November Barbara had talked Mom into letting them get a kerosene heater and use a cabin while they looked for a place to rent. Three months later they were still looking. Meanwhile, Roger was using a second cabin as a workshop, and Barbara had flowerpots outside the cabin door. Dad figured nothing short of dynamite would get them out.

I cut across the parking lot on my way to their place, my light bouncing as I walked. The only car in sight was the Batts' old VW bus, which was sitting at a funny tilt. I shone my light over there and saw that one side of the bus had been jacked up. Then I heard a giggle.

"Tony, Ricky," I called out, "what are you doing?"

Still giggling, the two of them dived under the bus. I ran forward. The jack was extended as high as it would go, holding both wheels on that side a good foot off the ground. The bus swayed back and forth.

I dropped to my knees and shone my light underneath. Ricky and Tony were sitting just out of reach, their tongues out.

"Get out from under there," I said. "This thing could come crashing down any second."

"You're not my boss," Ricky yelled. Tony laughed and wagged his tongue back and forth.

I wasn't about to go crawling after them. "Okay." I headed for the cabins. At the edge of the parking lot I turned my light back toward the bus. The boys were standing by the jack, rocking the bus up and down.

I ran up the path. Straight in front of me was Roger's workshop. White light flashed in the windows with each zap-zap of his welding torch.

"Roger," I yelled. "Come quick."

"Go away," he shouted.

I ran up and pounded on the door. "The boys are in trouble."

"Go tell Barbara and leave me alone."

I threw open the door. He was bending over a pile of metal, his back to me. His long black hair was tied back with some kind of string. "They're gonna get hurt."

"*You're* gonna get hurt," he yelled. "Get out and stay out."

"You're welcome." I spun around and dashed up the

path toward their cabin. "Barbara," I called. "Hey, Barbara."

She came strolling out the door. As usual, she was wearing one of those flowered dresses that looked like a tent.

"Tony and Ricky have the bus jacked up," I said. "I'm afraid it might fall on them."

She sighed, then smiled at me. "Thanks, Eddie."

I rushed back down the path, then had to stop and wait for her. I wondered why I was the one in a hurry.

When we reached the parking lot, I shone the light toward the bus, which was still rocking.

"Tony and Ricky," Barbara said, not raising her voice at all, "I want you to come and see me."

The two of them came running toward her. "Hi, Mommy salami," Tony said. They each grabbed one of her legs and buried their heads in her flowered skirt.

"I want to look at the bus," she said. Taking each of them by the hand, she led them across the lot. "You've certainly been busy, haven't you?"

"It wouldn't roll over," Tony said.

Ricky kicked his little brother for saying that.

Barbara stretched out her arms to hold them farther apart. "Ricky, do you know why you shouldn't do this?"

He shook his head, but that act wouldn't have fooled a three-year-old.

"That jack could slip, and the bus could fall right down on top of you. And that would flatten you like a pancake. Now we're going to put the bus down on the ground, and you're going to promise me not to play with the jack again."

Ricky broke free and ran to the jack. "Can I do it? Can I make it go down?"

Tony began to cry. "I want to. Please."

"You'll take turns." Barbara flipped the lever and then got Ricky started. Tony began to sob. "You'll get your turn."

"He's going to do it all," Tony blubbered.

"All right," Barbara said in a minute. "Now it's Tony's turn." Ricky kept working the handle. Barbara reached down, grabbed the back of his belt, and lifted him into the air. She held him there while Tony got started with the jack.

When the bus wheels were back on the ground, Barbara took apart the jack and stowed it in the rear of the bus. She kept the handle in her hand. "I think I'd better keep an eye on this for a while."

"Can we do it one more time?" Tony asked. "Please."

"No," she said. "I want you to go up to the house and take a bath."

"I don't want to," Ricky said.

"I know, but you're going to do it because I want you to."

"I get to sit in the front of the tub," Tony yelled, dashing toward the path.

"I get to." Ricky raced after him.

"This is a new one," Barbara said to me. "I had no idea they even knew what a jack was. I guess they've seen Roger use it."

"It scared me," I said. "That jack didn't look too steady. I tried to get Roger to come, but he wouldn't."

"Don't ever bother him when he's working," she said. "If there's a problem, come get me. Roger's a very creative person, and it's a terrible struggle to turn the vision he has in his mind into something concrete."

"Mmm." I wondered if she had taken a good look at that pile of junk in there.

"He's had a very painful life, but he's managed to keep growing. I think he'll do important things."

Not knowing how to answer that, I took the snapshot out of my pocket. "I found this today. I'm doing a report on the marina for my geography class, and I came across it." I held the flashlight on the picture for her.

"Oh," she said. "I can't believe it. It seems like a thousand years ago. Not even in this lifetime."

"I almost didn't recognize you. Your hair fooled me."

She laughed. "That hair. I thought I was gorgeous. Spent hours combing it."

"I guess things were a lot different around here in those days."

She handed me the picture. "Some. They're nicer now, I guess. I sort of liked it better before there was so much asphalt and cement, though." She took a step toward the cabin.

"Julie says you were a great waitress," I said.

"She was too little to know any better." Barbara took another step or two. "I'd better get up there before the boys let the tub run over. First, though, I think I'll hide this jack handle." She opened the door of the van and slid the handle up into the springs of the front seat.

I followed her up the path. "Doing this report is really interesting," I said. "You find out all kinds of things."

"Is that right?" Her voice was different, sharper than before.

"I didn't even know you'd worked here. Now I've been hearing all about you and Roger and his motorcycle." I waited, but she didn't say anything. "I guess you had things a little rough back then."

"What makes it your business?" she snapped. "We're having a hard enough time these days without somebody coming along and digging up all the dirt from the past."

My mouth dropped open. I had never seen Barbara angry before. "It's just a school report," I said, running to catch up with her. "I didn't mean to say something I shouldn't. I'm sorry."

"Yeah." She turned back toward me, her voice a little softer. "Look, Eddie, people are always ready to talk. They don't care whose lives they mess up. But I'm not going to run away. Let 'em talk. As far as I'm concerned, all that stuff is from another lifetime. I'm not even the same person."

"Sorry I brought it up."

"And leave Roger alone," she said, starting up the hill. "Things are hard enough for him as it is."

I stomped back toward the parking lot. What a crummy piece of detective work! I had managed to get Barbara mad without learning one stupid thing.

I wondered if it was worth a trip to the docks to call Wendy. The way my luck was going, I was bound to get the answering machine.

I stopped to check my pockets for change and heard the zap-zap of Roger's welding torch. But there was something else, too—footsteps. I shone my light toward the parking lot and saw somebody duck behind the Batts' bus.

For a good minute I stood on the path and tried to decide what to do. Should I cut through the trees and head for home? I couldn't yell for help. Roger wouldn't budge from his work, even if I were getting my throat slit.

But as time passed and nothing happened, I started getting less scared and more curious. Somebody was down there, and I wanted to know who.

I came down the path slowly, my light shining far ahead of me. When I was almost to the parking lot, I left the path and cut away from the bus. My feet sank in the sticky mud.

Once I was on the blacktop of the parking lot, I picked my escape route, then turned back and shone my light on the bus. Nothing moved.

"Who's over there?" I called out.

"Me." Pooch stepped out, shading his eyes from my light. He was wearing a T-shirt and shorts.

"Man, you scared me." I moved the light away from him.

"What's the matter, Eddie? You got a guilty conscience or something?" He headed toward me.

"What were you doing over there?"

"I was jogging on the docks, and I heard you carrying on up here. Came up to see what the trouble was."

"But what were you hiding for?"

Pooch laughed. "Just trying to go easy on you, Eddie. I heard you catching the devil from Barbara, and I figured you didn't need an audience." He made a clicking sound. "She was a little steamed-up there. What'd you do—insult one of her little angels?"

"Something like that."

"How was that boat show?" he asked. "You see anything new?"

I ended up walking with him all the way to his houseboat. Otherwise he would have hung around while I used the phone.

Not that it mattered.

Wendy's little sister answered and said that Wendy couldn't take any phone calls because she hadn't made up all the work she'd missed. "Who is this anyway?"

"Prince Charles," I told her. "Princess Di and I were hoping Wendy could baby-sit for us tomorrow night."

"I don't get it," she said, and slammed down the receiver.

It was one of those nights.

10

I was excited about meeting Wendy at the basketball game on Friday. A movie or a dance would have been better for our first date, but I wasn't complaining. At least we'd get to spend some time by ourselves. At school Wayne Parks was always hanging around.

Because Julie was a cheerleader, my parents usually went to the games. That night, though, Mom was getting things ready for a party at the restaurant, so I had to bum a ride with Jack and Julie. Jack said they didn't need a chaperon, but it was just talk. He always helped me when it mattered.

While we were waiting for Julie, I asked him about the one detail that was bothering me. "I'm supposed to meet her there," I said. "Do I meet her inside the gym or outside?"

"Do you have a date or not?"

"More or less."

Jack grinned and shook his head.

"Well, it's not that simple," I told him. "She can't go

out on dates, so she's coming with her parents, and I'm supposed to meet her."

Jack broke out laughing. "You're singing the freshman blues again, Eddie. Everything ends up half-baked."

"So where do I meet her on a half-baked date?"

"Inside," he said. "That way you won't have to pay for her ticket."

"I don't want to look like a cheapskate."

"Why hide the truth? Besides, her parents are bringing her, right? You don't want to meet her father, do you?"

"I don't know."

"Look, he'll just shake your hand and give you a dirty look. That's what freshman girls' fathers always do."

"Really?"

"So save the hassle and the money. Wait inside."

I ended up waiting right inside the door. When Wendy and her father came in, she was careful to keep things looking casual. She pretended not to notice me at first, then said, "Oh, hi, Eddie," and introduced me to her father as a boy in her algebra class. He shook my hand and gave me a dirty look.

For a minute I thought the three of us would end up sitting together, but her father decided not to join us in the student rooting section. Wendy and I found an empty bench in the bleachers and were alone for twenty or thirty seconds before two of her friends came along, then three of mine. Then some friends of theirs. And finally Wayne Parks squeezed into a spot on the bench behind us. All through the game he kept leaning forward and making comments like "Where's the ref keep his Seeing Eye dog during the game?"

Even if Wendy and I hadn't had an audience, we couldn't have done much talking. During every time-out the Los Cedros Spirit Band, sitting three rows behind us, blasted us off the benches with fight songs.

To top things off, Wendy's father sat across the aisle and stared at us all night. And the Los Cedros Panthers blew a six-point lead in the final minute and lost the game at the buzzer.

Before Wendy and I had our coats on, her father showed up beside us, mumbled, "Nice to meet you, Willy," and led her away.

The night could have been worse, I guess. I didn't break an ankle or choke on my popcorn or rip my pants. But I had a hard time being thankful for those small favors.

Saturday morning, while Julie and I decorated the restaurant, Jack went to the local flea market with some of the tools and fishing tackle we'd salvaged.

That afternoon I went by his place to see how much money we had made. He was in the garage, bent over the workbench. "Are we rich?" I called out.

"Not much action," he said without looking up. "Still too early for most people to think about fishing poles."

"What's my share?"

"Twelve bucks and three of these lamps." Five camp lanterns were lined up on the workbench. Jack had the back off a sixth one.

"You're supposed to sell stuff, not buy it."

"These were too good to pass up. Two bucks apiece."

"Do they work?"

He blew on a piece of metal and held it up to the light. "You think they'd sell for two bucks if they worked?"

"So you bought six broken lamps. With my money."

"We'll fix 'em and sell 'em for ten. Maybe more."

"Since you're my buddy, I'll make you a deal," I said. "I'll sell you my three right now. Two bucks apiece."

"I wouldn't want to cheat you," he said. "Besides, I need all the money I've got. Thursday's Valentine's Day."

I leaned against the pickup and watched him dismantle the lantern, setting pieces in a row on the bench. "I've been thinking about Valentine's Day. What do you think I should get Wendy?"

"Nothing."

"That'd be real class."

"You've just started going around with her. Give her a card. Or maybe a flower. Keep it simple."

"What about a box of candy?"

"Listen to the high roller talking." He held up a piece of brass. "Go in the house and get me some steel wool, will you? It's under the sink."

I went in the side door and down the hall. Jack's bedroom door was open far enough for me to see piles of clothes scattered across the floor. "Your room looks worse than mine," I yelled.

"Nobody appointed you bedroom inspector," he shouted.

When I came back with the steel wool, he spent a minute or two scrubbing furiously. Then he looked toward me. "If you want to blow her mind, get her a rose.

At Hayward's Nursery you can get a nice one with a couple of ferns on the side for two dollars. But it looks classy."

"How do I get it to her?"

"What do you want, messenger service? You walk up to her, hand her the flower, and say something clever like 'Happy Valentine's Day.' "

"With everybody around?"

"If you're scared, buy her a card and stick it in her book when nobody's looking."

I stood and watched him reassemble the lantern, piece by piece. When he was finished, it still didn't work.

"What a bargain," I said.

He shoved the lanterns toward the back of the cluttered workbench. "Don't worry. We can always sell 'em to somebody else." He plopped down on the garage floor and leaned against a tire of the pickup.

"Hey, Jack," I said, "you know that theory about your mom dumping your dad's body into the lake?"

"It's not a theory."

"I don't care what you call it. It's wrong."

He looked up at me, his lips tight. "And you can prove that, right?"

"Sort of."

"And what's that supposed to mean?"

I told him about my conversation with his mother, but he didn't look convinced when I was finished. "You should have seen the look on her face," I went on. "She wasn't just—"

He waved me away. "Let it go."

"I don't care whether you believe it or not," I said. "Nobody's that good an actress."

"All right," Jack said. "I know you believe it." He looked away and shrugged. "Who knows? Maybe it's possible."

"Take a look at this." I handed him the snapshot of the kitchen crew.

"This is an old one," he said. "Look at Julie. She was cute clear back then. A little skinny but cute all the same."

"Check the blonde next to your mom."

"What about her?"

"That's Barbara Batt."

He looked again. "Yeah, I guess it is. What about it?"

"This picture was taken nine years ago. Barbara worked here that summer. And she was still here in the fall. Roger was around too. Then suddenly they took off, and nobody saw them again until last November."

Jack looked up at me. "For a dumb guy you're a pretty good detective."

"I talked to Barbara the other night, asked her about the old days. She got mad and told me to mind my own business."

"Barbara?"

"That's right. Sort of makes you wonder, doesn't it?"

Jack got up slowly. "Start at the beginning. Tell me everything you heard about Barbara and Roger."

I gave him the whole business.

"Where'd you hear all this?"

"Mom, Opal, your mom."

"What about Pooch?"

"I didn't ask him."

"Why not? Juicy piece of gossip like this—I'll bet he knows every gory detail." He grabbed one of the lanterns and headed down the driveway.

"What are you doing with that thing?" I asked him.

"Pooch might want to buy it."

At the docks Woody was gassing up Dr. Jenkins's boat. Dr. Jenkins stood in the doorway of the store, talking to Pooch.

"Thirteen thirty-two," Woody called out. He replaced the gas cap and headed inside. Dr. Jenkins handed him a twenty-dollar bill. "Got any change? Running a little short." That was Woody's standard line. Like most coin collectors, he was always hoping somebody would pass him a real treasure.

"Sorry," Dr. Jenkins said. He studied the lures in the display case. "What do you recommend for today?"

Woody slapped the change on the counter and adjusted his straw hat. "Staying home."

"What?"

Woody closed the cash drawer. "Water's too muddy right now. You're wasting your time."

Dr. Jenkins stomped away from the counter. "Well, I guess we'll give it a try anyway."

"Have a good boat ride," Woody said. "That's all you're gonna get."

"You blew your chance on that one," Jack told Woody as soon as Dr. Jenkins started his engine. "You could have sold him some of your five-dollar specials."

Woody snorted and headed for the coffeepot.

"That's the famous Woodrow Hall sales technique," Pooch said. "Always treat your customer like he's garbage." He picked up a five-pound bag of flour in each hand and started doing arm exercises.

Woody turned his back and poured some coffee. Jack took my snapshot out of his pocket. "Hey, Woody, have you seen this?"

Woody slurped his coffee. "Who's in it? I can't see it without my glasses."

"The restaurant crew from a long time back. Do you remember when Barbara Batt worked here?"

"I guess," Woody said.

"Lemme see that thing," Pooch said. He set down the flour and took Woody's reading glasses off the shelf. He studied the picture for a minute, then started to grin. "I'll be darned. That's Julie. Boy, she's grown up."

"Look at the blonde," I said. "You recognize her?"

Pooch nodded. "That's Barbara. Little Bobbie we called her back then. Cute little thing. A real pistol."

"I didn't recognize her," I told him.

"She's sure changed," Pooch said. "I guess kids like hers would take the fire out of anybody."

I took the picture from him. "Somebody said Roger was around back then."

"Billy Goat." Pooch laughed and took off Woody's glasses. "That's what your grandpa used to call him. He had a big, long beard, see? Old Ed said he looked like a billy goat and smelled like one too."

A boat pulled up at the gas pumps. Woody looked out the window and had another slug of coffee. The driver of the boat sounded his horn. "You want me to get that?" I asked Woody.

"I got it." He took a long drink, then set down his cup

and ambled toward the door. "Keep your shirt on," he yelled.

Pooch pointed a finger at me. "Your grandpa thought little Bobbie was something special. He was on crutches by then. Couldn't get down the hill anymore. So your mom had him handling the cash register at the restaurant to give him something to do. He and Bobbie were always kidding around. It just about killed him when she started going off with Billy Goat on his motorcycle."

"Did Roger work around here?" Jack asked.

"Him? Work? Not that boy. All he ever did was sit around and read books and smoke those funny brown cigarettes."

"Marijuana?" I asked.

"Yep. He'd sit up there in the parking lot, waiting for Bobbie to get off work, and he'd smoke that stuff. Didn't hide it or anything. Didn't care who was around."

"I'll bet Mom didn't like that much," I said.

Pooch grinned. "You got that right. Everybody tried to talk to Bobbie, make her see what kind of a bum that guy was. But she'd get all teary-eyed and say it was her business. Finally your momma got old Ed and the rest to back off. Figured maybe Bobbie'd get tired of the boy if everybody'd leave them alone. But it didn't work. They ran off together all the same."

"When was this?" Jack asked. "Do you remember?"

Pooch closed his eyes and counted on his fingers. "Eight, ten years ago. Something like that."

"What time of year?" I asked. "Halloween? Thanksgiving?"

"What difference does it make?"

I shrugged. "My mom was just wondering. She

couldn't remember. Says her memory's not what it used to be."

Pooch smiled and ran his fingers through his hair. "Let's see here. It was a good while after the restaurant closed, I know that. Bobbie started collecting unemployment, see? That didn't sit right with old Ed. He figured if you collected unemployment, you ought to be out hustling for a job. But Bobbie was spending all her time with Billy Goat by then. They were off somewhere studying. Some religious stuff, I think."

"Like what?" Jack asked.

"How would I know? Some cockeyed stuff or other. There was a whole outfit of 'em, and they had big plans about going off to India. Bobbie said she'd send me a postcard from there." He grinned at me. "I never got it. Didn't expect to either."

Jack picked up the lantern he'd brought along and set it on the counter. "What do you think of that? Might come in handy over on your boat."

Pooch turned the lantern backward and forward. "Does it work?"

"No battery in it," Jack said.

"What if you put in a battery? Would it work then?"

"Put one in and see," Jack said, but he lifted the lantern out of Pooch's hands.

"Where you going with that thing?" Pooch said.

"You want to buy it before we put a battery in?" Jack asked.

"Not likely."

Jack shrugged. "Suit yourself. When the battery goes in, the price doubles."

Woody came in and rang up the sale on the cash

register. "Hey, Woodrow," Pooch said, "what's a lantern like this worth?"

Woody snorted. "From him? Not a cent."

Jack walked to the door. "Well, you had your chance."

"Don't go rushing off," Pooch said. "What price were you thinking of?"

"Six bucks now. Twelve when the battery goes in."

"I'll give you six if it works," Pooch said. "A dollar right now."

"You had your chance." Jack went out the door.

"Wait for me," I yelled.

"Tell him I'll go three bucks right now," Pooch said.

I caught up with Jack on the walkway. "Pooch says he'll give you three bucks for it. If you're not interested, I'll go get one of mine."

"I told you I'd fix 'em," Jack said. "I was just looking for some quick cash."

"Me too. I'm just not as piggy as you are."

Jack gave me a shove. "You learn some things?"

"A little, I guess. I think my grandfather's out of it. If he couldn't get up and down the hill, he probably wasn't hauling bodies around."

Jack shook his head. "Your grandfather? Since when was he a suspect?"

"Anything's possible," I said. "I'm still checking on *your* alibi. Where were you on the night of—"

"Let's go see Roger," Jack said. "I've got a few questions for him."

"Like what?"

"Like how he was going to pay for a trip to India. How's that for a starter?"

11

Tony and Ricky were kneeling beside a puddle at the far end of the parking lot. "What're you doing?" I called.

"None of your beeswax," Ricky yelled.

"Giving Sparky a bath," Tony shouted.

I wondered what Sparky was but didn't bother to ask.

From Roger's workshop came the ringing thuds of metal hitting metal. "Sounds like a chain gang," Jack said.

We went up the gravel path to the cabin door. Jack knocked, then opened the door when nothing happened. I followed him inside.

Roger was using a vise and a small sledgehammer to bend strips of metal. Sweat trickled down his forehead and dripped off his short black beard.

"What a mess," I muttered.

The cabin was filled with scraps of sheet metal and galvanized pipe and rusty bedsprings and coat hangers and pieces of car engines. In the middle of the mess

Roger was building a mountain of junk, with pipes sticking out and rolls of barbed wire and some shiny chrome hubcaps.

Roger spun the handle of the vise and took out a lopsided triangle. He held it up to the light, then tossed it into a pile. As he reached for another strip of metal, he said, "If you need something welded, give me a few days. I'm on the move right now."

"I just want to ask you something," Jack said.

Roger stuck the end of the strip into the vise and spun the handle. "Make it quick."

"It's about something that happened nine years ago."

"Beat it." Roger attacked the metal with his hammer. "I've got no time for that kind of game."

"It's not a game. I'm talking about serious business."

Roger brought the hammer down hard. "Get out of here."

"It's up to you," Jack said. "You can talk to me, or you can talk to the sheriff."

Roger spit in our direction. "Is that supposed to scare me? Forget it, man. I'm clean. I'm so clean I squeak." He finished shaping the metal strip into another crooked triangle without looking at us again.

"You remember August Bartolozzi?" Jack said.

"What's that?"

"August Bartolozzi. He lived on Willner Street in San Francisco."

"Never heard of him." Roger turned his back, pulled on his welder's helmet, and lit his torch. "Now beat it. You look at this flame, and you'll singe your eyeballs." His voice was muffled by the helmet.

"Come on, Roger," Jack said. "Give me a minute, and I'll explain."

"I'm busy." He waved the torch in our direction—just close enough to make us decide not to stick around.

Jack followed me out the door and closed it after him. "Your grandfather wasn't far off. Billy Goat's not a bad name for him."

"You have any idea what he's making in there?" I asked.

"A mess," Jack said.

We walked back toward the parking lot. "If he was worried, he did a good job of hiding it," I said.

Jack shook his head. "I know. He didn't even blink when I mentioned Bartolozzi."

"Now what?"

Jack sat down on a log beside the parking lot. "Maybe Barbara will be easier."

We sat on the log for more than half an hour, waiting for Barbara. During that time I learned two things: (1) Jack didn't have any better theories than I did, and (2) Sparky was an earthworm.

When Barbara drove in, the boys raced toward the bus. Jack and I stood back while they each hugged her. "You want to hug Sparky, too?" Tony yelled, shoving the worm in Barbara's face.

"Nice Sparky," she said, giving it a pat. "Where'd he come from?"

"We found him on the hillside. Ricky had one, too, but his fell apart."

"Ricky," Barbara said, "what's in your mouth?"

Ricky backed away. "Nothing."

"You have something there. I can tell."

He turned away and swallowed. Then he turned back and showed her his empty mouth. "I don't have anything. See?"

She took hold of his arm. "You had something. I saw it." She pulled him close. "Let me smell your breath. Come on. Breathe out." She stood and waited until he finally had to exhale. "Bubble gum. I knew it. Who gave it to you?"

"Nobody."

"Tell the truth, honey. I know you had bubble gum. Who gave it to you?"

A smile crossed Ricky's face. "Nobody gave it to me. And I'm not lying."

"Where'd you find it?" she asked.

"Under the picnic table down there." He pointed toward the campground.

"You mean it was already chewed?"

Ricky nodded. "But it still had flavor."

"You know we don't allow gum," she said. "You go up to the house right now."

"I didn't chew gum," Tony told her.

"Good," she said. "You get to carry the groceries." She handed him a large brown bag.

He trotted across the parking lot. "I get to carry the bag," he yelled.

Ricky turned back and showed his tongue.

"Barbara," I said, "can we bother you for a second?"

Judging by the look she gave me, I could have been the one chewing secondhand gum. "What is it?"

"We want to talk about that summer you worked here," Jack said.

Barbara glared at him, then at me. "Well, I don't."

She took a few steps away from the bus. "Why are you doing this, Eddie? I don't understand it at all."

"Come on, Barbara," Jack said. "We're not going to make trouble for anybody. We've got this problem. If you'd just give us a few minutes, we could get everything straightened out."

"A problem? About that?"

"Right," Jack said.

Barbara closed her eyes and took a deep breath. She held it for a long time, then let it go with a puff. "Relaxation training," she said, almost smiling. "Look, I'm tired, and my family is hungry. If you absolutely *have* to talk to me, come back about nine. But first think it over and be sure it's necessary." Then she did smile. "Fair enough?"

"You bet," I told her.

We stood by the bus while she walked up the gravel path. "I've thought it over," Jack said, "and it's necessary."

Jack came by my house a little before nine. I brought along my flashlight, but we didn't use it walking down to the parking lot.

"This is messing up my love life," Jack said. "I was supposed to take Stephanie Daniels to the movies tonight. When I called her and said I had to work late, I got the old deep freeze treatment."

"Did you cancel the whole thing?"

"No, we're still going out for pizza later, but Stephanie didn't sound too thrilled about it."

The light was on in Roger's workshop, and we could

hear him pounding metal again. "Think we ought to stop by and say hello?" I asked.

"Not unless you want to be part of the sculpture," Jack said.

Barbara was sitting on her front step beneath the porch light. She had a blanket wrapped around her shoulders. "You decided it's absolutely necessary?" she asked.

"Afraid so," Jack said.

"Somehow I thought you would." She tucked the blanket around her knees. "I'd offer you some tea, but I don't want to go back inside. I just put the boys to bed."

"That's all right," I said. I had tried her tea before—herbal stuff that was sort of like drinking hot salad. We weren't missing much.

"Now, what's the problem?"

"We need to know about the fall after you worked here," Jack said.

Barbara looked up at him and shook her head. "You've heard the stories, I guess. I thought maybe after nine years people would forget. But I should have known better."

"You remember a guy named August Bartolozzi?" Jack asked her.

"No. Was he around here then?"

"I think so."

"I don't remember him. But that whole time's kind of fuzzy. What's he have to do with us?"

"I thought maybe he was Roger's partner."

"I don't get it." Barbara's voice rose higher. "What does any of this have to do with you? Roger went to prison. So what? Why's that any of your business?"

Jack and I stood and looked at each other.

"Momma," one of the boys called from inside, "can I have something to eat?"

"No," Barbara said.

"I can't go to sleep. My stomach's too empty."

"It's not empty, honey. It's lonely. Tell it a story." She stood up. "I guess we're keeping them awake. Let's move away a little." She walked about thirty feet down the gravel path. Jack and I followed along. "I want to stay close enough so I can still hear them," she whispered. "Now, Eddie, what's this all about?"

I couldn't answer her.

"We didn't know anything about Roger's being in prison," Jack said.

"I'm surprised," she said. "I figured that'd be big news on the hot line around here."

"I never heard it," I told her.

"It's no big secret. We were young and stupid. We wanted to make a killing and go off to India."

Jack moved a step closer to her. "We heard about India."

"Stay away from drugs," Barbara told us. "They mess up your mind. Here's how bad off we were. We got an old truck and headed for L.A. with cardboard boxes full of pot. Gonna make a bundle and go to India. You'd think we'd be really careful, right? Not us. We went straight down the freeway in broad daylight. Stopped at one of the rest stops. And listen to this. Roger was sitting on the tailgate of the truck, drinking lemonade, and he lit up a joint. That's how far out of touch we were."

"What happened?" I asked after a minute.

"Cop spotted him. Busted both of us. They let me go the next day because Roger told them I was a hitchhiker he'd picked up. But Roger spent over three years in prison. Three years. You never get over something like that. Not really. For a long time he couldn't do anything. Just sat around. Now, after all these years, he's getting back to himself, doing great work—powerful things."

"We didn't know any of this," I said.

Barbara shivered. She wrapped the blanket around her shoulders again. "It's all hard to believe. We were so young and so incredibly stupid."

"Momma," Ricky yelled, "my stomach is still hungry. Can I get a cracker?"

"I'll get it for you." She moved past us. "I'll be right back."

"What do you think?" I whispered once she had gone inside.

"Looks bad," Jack said. "Unless Roger had another plan to finance that trip."

Barbara came back outside carrying her wallet. "I keep this around," she said. "It's a good reminder never to take things for granted." She pulled out a newspaper article that had been folded into a two-inch square. She unfolded it carefully.

I turned on my flashlight and read the headline: POT DEALER ARRESTED BY ALERT DEPUTY. I read enough of the story to see Roger's name. I would have read more, but my eyes kept moving back to the date at the top of the paper: October 25—two days before the bank robbery.

"Check the date," Jack whispered.

"I saw it."

Barbara folded the article slowly, then slid it into a back compartment of the wallet. "Some things you can't afford to forget." She closed the wallet and turned to me. "Now, what's going on?"

"It was a mistake," I started.

"It was something to do with my father," Jack said, "but it happened after you left. Do you want all the details?"

"Not really," Barbara said.

"Sorry to bother you," Jack told her.

"Don't worry," I said. "We won't tell anybody about this."

"No problem, Eddie. We're not trying to hide. When we decided to come back here, we figured people would know."

"Momma," Tony yelled, "he keeps bothering me."

"He's a liar," Ricky said.

Barbara started for the cabin. "I'd better go settle them down."

"See you later," Jack said.

"Good night, Barbara," I called after her.

Jack and I walked down the path. "Back to square one," I muttered.

"Looked good for a little while," he said.

"Where do we go from here?"

Jack started across the parking lot. "Well, one of us is going off to have pizza with Stephanie Daniels."

"You know what I mean."

"Do me a favor, Eddie. Forget about the whole thing."

"Oh, sure."

"Look, make a list. See what you end up with. Your grandfather and Opal were too sick. Your dad was gone. Besides my mom, all you have left is your mom, Woody, and Pooch. You figure one of them was mixed up in a bank robbery?"

"Not really."

"So I want you to quit asking questions before my mom hears about it. I don't want to worry her."

"Okay," I said. "Enjoy your pizza."

He headed for home, and I jogged down to the docks to call Wendy.

Somebody picked up the phone in the middle of the first ring. "Hello. Westfall residence." It was Wendy's little sister.

"Hello. Is Wendy there?"

"No. Is this Prince Charles again?"

"Right. Do you know when she'll be back?"

"Not till late. She's at a party at Wayne Parks's house."

My stomach turned over. I felt as if I had just swallowed a king-size anchovy pizza—whole. "Thanks anyway," I managed to mumble.

"Who are you really? I know you aren't Prince Charles."

"I'm Santa Claus. I just wanted to make sure you liked all your presents."

"Very funny."

"See you next Christmas," I said, and hung up.

12

On Sunday afternoon I hauled the shoeboxes of pictures and brochures into my bedroom. My project was due in two weeks, and I hadn't written a word. Julie sat on my floor and looked through pictures for a while. I told her about the false alarm with the Batts.

"It's a good thing you have that San Diego alibi," I said. "Otherwise you'd be number-one suspect. Everybody else seems to be eliminated."

Julie set a stack of pamphlets on the floor. "You know, it wouldn't be a big tragedy if you just gave up the whole thing."

"If I don't do this report, I don't pass geography."

"I don't mean the report. Go ahead and do that. I mean the detective business."

"That's what Jack says, but that's because he thinks his mom did it."

"Maybe she did."

"I'd bet anything she didn't."

"Maybe she had reasons you don't know anything

about. You'd better quit before you end up hurting somebody."

"Look, Julie, there's a skeleton at the bottom of Muir Lake, and somebody around here probably put it there. How am I supposed to forget something like that?"

"You want nice, simple answers," she said. "Sometimes things don't work that way."

"What about the bone and the license plate under Jack's bed? Do we just pretend they don't exist?"

Julie slid the pictures off her lap and stood up. "Would you rather hurt somebody?"

"Maybe I ought to tell Vince and let him take care of it."

Julie looked down at me. "Promise me you won't do that, Eddie."

"What's wrong?"

"Just promise, all right?"

I waved her away. "Vince'd probably laugh in my face anyway."

"Thanks, Eddie."

"Hey, before you go, give me a flashy opening for my paper. Once I get a start on this baby, I think I'll be all right."

She stood in the doorway and thought for a minute. "How's this? 'Grizzly Creek Marina, once a run-down fishing resort, has become a gathering place for the rich and famous of the world.' "

"You're a big help."

"Take your choice," she said. "Truth or flash. You can't have both."

I settled for truth—a dippy sentence that said, "Grizzly Creek Marina has seen many changes through the years."

By Tuesday night I had finished all the early history and was plowing toward the present. The only problem was that I had done it all in less than two pages. I was hoping that if I put in enough pictures, Mr. Crowell wouldn't count words.

I kept running across pictures of Pooch and his new houseboat. I wondered if maybe we hadn't eliminated him too quickly. He seemed harmless enough, but so did everybody else around there. I wondered where Pooch had found the money for that boat. But if he had been mixed up in something illegal, why call attention to himself by buying something like that?

I took a break from my report and wandered into the living room. Dad was reading his *Runner's World* while Mom wrote letters. "Mom," I said, "where did Pooch get the money for his houseboat?"

"He inherited it."

"From who?"

"From whom," Mom said. "I'm not sure. Somebody said it was an aunt. Somebody else said a sister."

Dad looked up. "Pooch never did settle for one story. He told some people he'd made a killing in the stock market. And then he claimed he'd hit it big in Reno."

Mom smiled. "Pooch always did like a good story. I'm pretty sure he inherited it, though."

I went back to my room, wondering if I had learned anything.

While I worked on the project, I tried to decide what to give Wendy for Valentine's Day. I had the twelve dollars from the flea market, so for once money wasn't a problem.

I just didn't know where I stood with her. She was friendly enough, but I had the sick feeling that I was number two on her list. Whenever I joined her group outside the algebra room, Wayne Parks was right in the middle, talking about his car or some college he was going to visit.

I hadn't touched the phone since Saturday night. Whenever I thought about calling, I remembered Arthur Prentice, a guy who was always calling Julie and sending her presents. Whenever he called, Julie would wave for one of us to yell at her or ring the doorbell so that she could say she had to go. "He's a perfectly nice guy, and I don't want to hurt his feelings," she'd say, "but he's a pest."

I didn't want to be another Arthur Prentice.

But sometimes in algebra Wendy would look back at me and smile, and I'd tell myself there might be hope after all.

On Wednesday afternoon, the thirteenth of February, I still hadn't made up my mind. Jack dropped Julie at the card shop, then drove over to Hayward's Nursery and Florist. On the way, I tried to explain my problem.

Jack listened, then said, "You know what your trouble is? NG."

"NG?"

"No guts. Look, a while back you said you were in love. You change your mind?"

"No."

"Then give it your best shot, dummy."

"But it may not—" I said.

"What do you expect? You think the flower people here are going to give you a money-back guarantee? Either she falls madly in love with you, or you get your chintzy two bucks back?"

"I'm sorry I brought it up," I said. But I wasn't.

At Hayward's I rushed inside before I lost my nerve. And I bought three roses instead of one.

Jack hid his bouquet behind the seat so that Julie wouldn't see it. "Could you put mine there, too?" I asked him.

"What's the matter?"

"I don't want Julie to know about this."

"Why not? You ought to be proud."

I couldn't explain it. "Just help me out, okay?"

Jack grinned. "No problem. You want me to keep them in our refrigerator tonight?"

"Would you do that? Thanks, Jack."

"That's all right. I was a dippy freshman once too." He couldn't let it go there. He had to add, "Not as dippy as you, though."

When we got home, I worked on my report for about ten minutes, then walked down to the marina. After buying the flowers, I was too wound up to concentrate.

Woody was standing outside the store, looking at the fishing blackboard, which was up for the first time since last summer. The fishing was listed as "fair," which was as low as Woody would go. Under "Recommended bait," he had drawn a large question mark. While I watched, he erased the question mark and drew it again a little larger. He took a step back and examined it.

"I liked it better the other way," I said, trying to get a rise out of him.

"It was crooked," he said.

"So's this one. You want me to draw it for you?"

"Get out of here." But he erased it and started over.

Inside the store Pooch was playing with the television set Woody keeps on the upper shelf for football games. "Stupid TV," he said. "Must be a hundred years old."

"What's on?"

"Quiz show." The sound blared, but the black-and-white picture kept rolling. "I get kind of a kick out of it."

"Why don't you watch it at your place?"

Pooch glared at me. "Do you think I'd be fooling with this antique of Woodrow's if I had any choice? I had to haul my set to the shop today, and those robbers wouldn't fix it while I was there." He banged on the top of the set. "If they let you watch 'em work, they couldn't lie about how long it took."

Woody opened the door and yelled, "Quit hitting that thing."

"Look what it's doing," Pooch said. "It just keeps rolling."

"It worked fine till you started messing with it." Woody stomped in and put the chalk and the eraser into the box under the counter.

"Old Woodrow's something," Pooch said to me. "Opal's TV was about as old as this one. The picture started getting littler and littler, but Woodrow kept saying it was fine. If Franklin hadn't sent her a new TV, she'd be up there watching a two-inch picture." He banged on the set again. "What good is a TV if it doesn't work?"

"I'll fix it." Woody pushed Pooch out of the way, then reached up and turned off the set. "See? No problems."

Pooch shook his head. "Fifty-one years old, and you're still having tantrums."

"Get out of my store, you old fool," Woody shouted.

Pooch smiled and leaned against the freezer. "Woodrow gets too excited," he said to me. "That's why his hair fell out."

Woody locked the cash register, shoved the key in his pocket, and headed for the door.

"That's real bright, Woodrow," Pooch said. "How am I supposed to wait on somebody if the register's locked?"

"I don't want you near that register. You'd probably break it." He tugged on his hatbrim and marched out.

"Ornery today, ain't he?" Pooch switched on the set, then picked up a sack of flour and held it straight out in front of him. "Grab a sack, and we'll have a contest for a dollar. First one to put it down loses."

"You go ahead and warm up for ten or fifteen minutes while I think about it." I walked over and turned off the TV. "That was making me seasick."

"Grab a sack," he said. "I'll still beat you."

I leaned against the counter. I had just about given up detective work, but I couldn't help being curious. "Hey, Pooch, a kid at school said his dad paid over fifty thousand for a houseboat. You figure that's true?"

"He could have paid a lot more than that."

"Really? Could a guy get a loan for something like that?"

Pooch's arms were starting to shake. "Probably."

"Did you finance yours?"

"Nope."

"You mean you paid cash?"

"That's right."

I let out a whistle. "Wow. Where'd you get all the money?"

Pooch set the sack on the counter and took a deep breath. "Here and there."

"Come on, Pooch. Where'd it come from?"

"What's with all the questions? You running your own quiz show?"

I waited awhile, hoping he'd go ahead and answer, but he just walked around and flexed his arms. Finally I said, "Somebody told me your aunt left you some money."

"Don't believe everything you hear."

"It wasn't your aunt, huh?"

Pooch bent over and touched his toes. "Nosy bug bit you bad, didn't it?"

"What's the big secret?"

"Since when do you start asking people about their money?"

"Don't get mad, Pooch. I was just talking."

Pooch grabbed his sweatshirt and headed for the door. "You were just poking your nose into other people's business."

"Take it easy," I said, but he kept going. Figuring I had nothing to lose, I gave him one more shot. "What's the matter? You got some secrets you're hiding?"

He turned back and pointed a finger at my chest.

"You'd better watch yourself." Then he spun around and left.

It was a good thing that I was giving up detective work. I was lousy at it.

Jack was at our house that night. He and Julie sat at the kitchen table and did their physics homework. When they finished their last problem, Jack slammed his book shut. "Let's celebrate by taking a ride into town."

"Go ahead," Julie said. "I'm going to celebrate by doing my Spanish and ironing some clothes."

"Wild times at Grizzly Creek Marina," Jack said.

I caught him on the way out. "Hey, Jack, how about going down to the docks for a minute? I want to show you something."

"It's a lousy second choice," he said, but he came along.

The night was clear and cold. Frost was already forming on the windshield of Jack's truck. He opened the door and tossed his books on the seat. "Are we riding or walking?"

"Save your gas," I said. "I just wanted to tell you something."

He slammed the door. "What's going on?"

"Look, I know you didn't want me asking any more questions, but something came up today." I told him about Pooch and the houseboat.

When I was through, Jack gave me a shove. "You never quit, do you?"

"I didn't think it'd hurt. I was just curious. I didn't expect him to get mad."

"It's probably nothing," Jack said, leaning against the truck.

"I know. It just seemed kind of funny."

After we had stood there for a minute or two, Jack said, "Oh, well, we might as well see what Pooch has to say for himself."

We were coming down the hill when we spotted Pooch in front of the lighted store. He turned on a flashlight and started across the walkway.

"That's nice," I said. "He's coming to meet us."

I flipped on my light so that Pooch would see us coming. We waited for him at the end of the walkway.

"Hello, Pooch," Jack called out.

"Evenin'." He came off the walkway without slowing down.

"What's your hurry?" Jack asked.

"Going up to see a program at Opal's. My TV's in the shop."

"We were just coming to see you," Jack said. "I had a couple of things I wanted to ask you about."

"Like what?" Pooch sounded peeved.

"Oh, just some stuff about the old days," Jack said.

Pooch turned his light on me. "You at it again?"

I raised my hand in front of my eyes. "What do you mean?"

"Poking into other people's business."

"He's just doing a report for school," Jack said.

Pooch waved us away. "I know what goes in a school report and what doesn't." He started up the hill. "I've got a show to see."

"Hey, Pooch," Jack called after him, "did Eddie read

you the chapter about August Bartolozzi and the bank?"

Pooch kept walking.

"You sure that was smart?" I asked Jack.

"Didn't hurt anything. If he's clean, it didn't mean a thing. If he isn't, maybe it'll shake things loose."

Seeing somebody in the store, we wandered across the walkway. Woody had an outboard engine sitting on the counter.

Jack stuck his head in the door. "What's the matter? Don't you get enough of this place in the daytime?"

"Lousy soap operas," Woody said. "Bad enough they watch 'em all day. Now the stupid things come on at night. And Momma's got that TV turned up so high you can't get away from it."

Jack and I came inside and stood by the heater. "You don't like soap operas?" Jack asked.

"Enough filth and misery in the world without getting it off the TV." Woody picked up a screwdriver and a wrench.

"You want me to hold that steady for you?" Jack said.

Woody shrugged. "As long as you're not doing anything."

While the two of them argued about whether the prop was bent, I went outside and called Wendy. For once she answered the phone.

"Hi, Wendy," I said. "I was afraid I'd get the machine again."

"I'll tell you about that sometime."

"How many people are listening to every word you say?"

"Three. I'm still doing my Spanish, so I can't talk long."

I caught myself thinking of poor old Arthur Prentice.

We talked about the basketball team and the algebra homework. Then she said, "I have to go."

"Listen," I blurted, "I have a valentine for you."

She laughed. "You better have. I have one for you. See you tomorrow."

I was grinning when I went back inside the store. Maybe I was number two, but at least I wasn't in Arthur Prentice's class.

For the next hour I stood by the heater while Jack and Woody worked over the motor. They argued a little about how to adjust the carburetor, but most of the time they worked without talking. I probably would have had a more interesting time up at Opal's watching filth and misery.

A few minutes before ten we put things away and locked up the place. Jack and I followed Woody across the walkway, then rode up the hill in his truck. He let us off at my mailbox.

"I think we'd better have another talk with Pooch," Jack said.

"He may not feel like talking," I said.

"That's tough. Either he knows something, or he doesn't. And I'm going to find out which."

"Good luck," I muttered.

We waited by Woody's mailbox until Pooch came down the driveway. "How was the show?" Jack asked.

"Okay." Pooch flashed his light on us. "What're you two doing out here?"

"Waiting for you," Jack said.

"What for?"

"Wanted to ask you a couple of things, Pooch." Pooch started to say something, but Jack cut him off. "Just hold on a second, will you? I'm trying to find out about my father. Seems like he was mixed up in some funny business before he took off."

"I don't know nothing about it," Pooch said.

"He and a guy named August Bartolozzi were in a bank in San Francisco on October twenty-seventh. That bring back any memories?"

"Nope," Pooch said, heading down the road. We walked along beside him for a minute. I wondered if I was supposed to ask the next question.

Finally Jack said, "Somebody here got mixed up in this business. Eddie and I aren't going to make any trouble. We just want to clear up some loose ends. And you can help."

"I don't know what you're talking about," Pooch said.

"Here's the way it is, Pooch. This funny business is tied up with money. So we get really interested when people suddenly come up with money they didn't have before. See what I mean?"

"I don't know about any funny business," Pooch said.

"I believe you, Pooch, because I know what kind of guy you are. But somebody that didn't know you might wonder where you got the money to buy that house-boat."

Pooch stopped walking and turned his light on us. "That's what you want to know, isn't it? That's what this whole thing's about. Well, it's none of your stinkin' business. I got that money perfectly legal, and that's all in the world you need to know. Now leave me alone."

Pooch marched down the hill without saying another word. Jack tried to kid him along, even tried apologizing. But Pooch just kept walking.

Jack and I stopped at the water's edge and watched him stamp across the walkway. "Contrary old coot," Jack said. "I'm sick of sitting around and wondering. I'm going up and get that license plate. Then I'll go out there and stick it under his nose."

"You think that's smart?"

"I don't care if it's smart or not," Jack said. "I'm tired of wasting time." He went trotting up the hill.

I stood around and tossed a few rocks into the lake. Then I did some jumping jacks to keep warm, but they didn't help much. I checked my watch and saw that fifteen minutes had gone by. After another five minutes I headed back up the hill. I was almost to our mailbox when I spotted Jack coming down the road.

"What happened to you?" I called out.

He didn't answer until he was standing in front of me. "This is really weird, Eddie."

"What are you talking about?"

"The bag's gone."

13

The next morning I stood by the window and watched for Jack's pickup, then rushed out to meet him. He looked terrible. His face was splotchy, and he had purple circles around his eyes. "I still think it could have been Pooch," I said. "He saw us with the plastic bag that first day."

"It could have been the tooth fairy too." Jack climbed out of the truck with his bouquet in his arms.

"You can't be absolutely sure. Pooch could have—"

"Drop it, Eddie. The only two guys I'm absolutely sure didn't take it are you and Grandma Woody. But we both know my mom did it. So do me a favor and forget the whole thing, all right?"

"You didn't talk to her, did you?"

"Be serious. What would I say?" He turned toward me, holding his bouquet up against his shoulder, the way he might hold a baby. "Look, that stuff's history. This is Valentine's Day, and we've got some fantastic flowers for the women we love. Let's enjoy it."

"Good idea."

"Your flowers are there on the floorboard. Don't step on 'em."

I glanced toward the house. "I think I'll just put them behind the seat for now."

While I stowed away my bouquet, Jack carried his to our door. Julie just happened to be there waiting. She took the flowers and kissed him all in one movement. I wished I could get a reception like that from Wendy.

Julie had to find a vase for the flowers, so we were later than usual. Then, just past our mailbox, we met Vince Minetti, who signaled for us to stop. We pulled up beside his patrol car, and he rolled down the window.

"Hey, Jackie," he yelled, "found any Model As lately?" He laughed and smacked a big fist on the steering wheel.

"Happy Valentine's Day," Jack said.

"I heard a new one the other day, Jackie. Guy said there was a Model A down a mine shaft over by Parker Lake. Maybe you'd better check it out." He laughed and smacked the wheel again.

"See you," Jack said, letting out the clutch.

"Keep looking, Jackie."

When we got to school, Jack and Julie went racing for class. As soon as Julie disappeared through the door, I reached behind the seat for my bouquet.

The final bell rang.

I was late again, but at least the hallway was empty. Even so, I kept the flowers hidden behind my books. I got almost to Mr. Crowell's classroom, then decided I couldn't take the bouquet in there. For a minute I thought about dumping it in a trash can and forgetting the whole thing.

Not knowing what else to do, I headed down the hall and stuffed the flowers into my locker. That solved my problem for the moment.

Before I went to algebra, I stopped by the locker. I stood there like an idiot and stared at the bouquet. Then I slammed the locker door.

Jack was right: NG.

Wendy was standing outside the room with three other people. One of them was Wayne Parks, naturally.

"Happy Valentine's Day," she said, handing me a red envelope.

"Thank you," I said.

She looked down at my books, obviously expecting one from me.

Right then I wished I had bought a card instead of a stupid bouquet. Not as classy maybe, but a lot easier to deliver.

"Open it," Wayne said. "They're neat." I realized that everybody else was holding a red envelope like mine.

"Go ahead," Wendy said. "It's kind of sloppy sentimental, but that's okay."

Wendy had made the card herself. On the front she had drawn a tough-looking woman with huge tattooed arms. Inside was the verse:

Forget that stuff
About hearts and lace.
Be my Valentine
Or I'll break your face.

It was signed "Love and stuff, Wendy."

"That's great," I said.

While the card was being passed around, Miss Lennox came to the door and waved us inside. Wendy looked toward my books again.

"It's in my locker," I told her.

"What's the matter? Is it too mushy to give me in public?"

"Something like that."

"Now you've got me curious. Let's get it right after class."

I didn't learn much algebra that hour.

When Wendy and I came out the door afterward, Wayne was waiting in the hall. He ducked between people to move next to Wendy. "You should have seen what happened in Bell's class—"

Wendy put her hand on his shoulder and said, "You'll have to excuse us, Wayne. Eddie and I have to run get something."

We were gone before he could say another word.

At my locker I dropped my books on the floor and turned the dial. Mr. Crowell was walking up the hall toward us.

Jerry Bridges stopped next to me. "Hey, Eddie, did you see that basketball game on TV last night?"

"Give me a second, Jerry," I said. "Wendy and I were—"

"It was fantastic," Jerry went on. "Tie game with seventeen seconds to go. Then there were two turnovers in the next nine seconds. So it was still tied with eight seconds left, and neither team had a time-out left."

I turned the dial back to sixteen, lifted the handle, and jerked the locker door open. Wendy let out an "Oh" and reached for the roses. Then she spun around and planted a kiss on me—right there in front of Jerry Bridges and Mr. Crowell and everybody.

"Crimeny," Jerry said, and walked off.

Mr. Crowell grinned and looked away.

I just stood there with a stupid smile on my face, too far gone even to say, "Happy Valentine's Day."

After school we had to stop by Hayward's Nursery, which had called that morning to say that there were flowers there for Julie. (The deliveryman wouldn't go all the way to the marina, especially not on Valentine's Day.)

Julie already had a paper bag full of cards and several boxes of candy sitting on her lap. "It's a good thing I'm not the jealous type," Jack said, eyeing all her loot.

"That's right," she said. "If you were, I wouldn't share my candy with you." She opened a box and held it out to him.

Jack took two big pieces. "I don't really want these, but I'd hate for you to think I was mad."

"It's amazing," I said. "All day I kept expecting somebody to come up and give me a flower or a box of candy, and nobody did. I can't understand it."

"Have a box of candy." Julie shoved one toward me.

"I'm too proud to take secondhand stuff," I told her.

"Don't feel bad," she said. "I have something at home for you."

Hearing that, I went into Hayward's to get a card for her. All the funny cards were gone, but I found a really tacky lace one that said "For Sister Dear" on the front. Inside was a poem so sloppy you had to either laugh or get sick. It was perfect.

Hayward's had three big bouquets for us—two of them for Julie from guys who were away at college. The third was for Opal, sent by her boy Franklin. Opal's bouquet was the biggest of the three. "That's the trouble with college boys," Jack said. "Bunch of cheapskates."

The pickup started making funny noises five miles from home. Jack slowed down and nursed it along, hanging his head out the window to listen to the engine. "This could make a big dent in my Valentine's Day plans," he muttered.

I didn't want to compete with the soap operas, so I waited until four o'clock to take Opal's flowers to her. "Come on in," she yelled before I had a chance to knock.

She was sitting in her recliner, wearing her bathrobe and floppy slippers. "Here you go." I handed her the bouquet. "These are really something. Don't tell her I told you, but none of Julie's boyfriends sent her flowers this neat."

Opal laughed and hauled herself out of the chair. "That Franklin, he spoils me." She stood for a minute to catch her breath, then padded off to the kitchen to get a vase. "Come give me a hand."

I dug through her cupboard but couldn't find a vase. We ended up putting the flowers in a pitcher. I put water in the pitcher, then carried it in and set it on the table beside Opal's recliner. She sank down in the chair and said, "Have a piece of candy."

Next to the pitcher was a box of chocolates with most of the top layer gone. I studied the candy carefully, hoping to get one that didn't have pineapple glop inside. "Another valentine, huh?"

Opal laughed. "That crazy Pooch. He left it on my front porch, then called on the phone to say it was there. He was afraid to come in and give it to me." She reached out and grabbed the piece of candy I had just decided to take. "He's always making big talk, but I know better than to pay any attention."

I picked a dark brown piece. "What's the matter? He's not your type?"

Opal popped the candy into her mouth. "He's nobody's type. That Pooch is a bachelor through and through. Him and his exercises. Nobody could stand to be around him very long. I tell you, Eddie, there's two kinds of men in the world—marryin' men and bachelor types. And I don't want either kind."

I bit down on my candy. It had orange cream in the middle. I held it in my mouth, wondering how to spit it out without Opal catching me. "Is that right?" I mumbled.

"The bachelors all think they want to be married, but they're not cut out for it. Woody's father was like that. We got divorced after five years, both of us glad to get out from under. He had no more business being married than old Pooch." She glanced over at me and laughed. "What's the matter, Eddie? You get one of those awful-tasting ones? Don't swallow it, for heaven's sake." She handed me a Kleenex, and I got rid of the candy. "I don't know where Pooch got this stuff. Probably on sale at the Bonanza Eighty-eight-Cent Store."

She pushed the box toward me again. "You don't think you'd like living on a houseboat, huh?" I was just making talk while I studied the candy.

"Not on your life. Besides, Pooch wouldn't want anybody on his boat. His idea of the perfect marriage would be for him to stay down on his boat and show up here for mealtime. I'm telling you, Eddie, one bachelor around here is plenty for me. I just thank heaven Woody never got married. He's not cut out for it either."

"Woody's never been married, huh?" I finally took a chance on a light brown square. Caramel inside. Nobody loses every time.

"Nope. There was a woman about five years back that had her eye on him, but it didn't work out. She was lucky. A woman gets desperate, see? She figures any man would be better than being alone. And that's wrong. Pooch's wife found that out."

"Pooch's wife? Was he married?"

Opal leaned back in her chair and laughed. "For a little while. That old rascal, he thinks it's a big secret. But I heard the story a little while back. A woman from Los Cedros was a sister to the woman who lived right down the street from Pooch's wife. Yep, old Pooch was married, and he was just as rotten a husband as you'd figure."

"When was this?"

"Oh, this was years and years ago. There was an old maid down in Lincoln Springs, worked in the post office. Ugly as a mud fence, I hear. Anyway, she got up in her forties or so, and Pooch started coming around. I guess she figured he was better than nothing." Opal glanced over at me. "Was that second piece any better?"

"It was good," I said.

"Have another one." She shoved the box toward me, but I waved it away. I was quitting while I was ahead. "Anyhow, right after they got married, Pooch quit his job and couldn't seem to find anything else. He thought he'd found himself a good deal. She'd make the money, and he'd spend it. That's his idea of teamwork. Well, pretty soon the old gal decided that if this was marriage, then being single wasn't such a bad life after all. She booted him out, and that was it."

"No wonder he doesn't tell anybody."

"That rascal came out winners all the same. The old gal never got around to divorcing him, so when she died, Pooch got her house and whatever else she had, and he's been living in the high cotton ever since."

There went my last suspect. "Is that right?"

"Don't say anything about this," Opal said. "The woman that told me is going to get me a picture of Pooch's wife. Then when he starts talking about money smarts the way he does, I'm going to haul out the picture and say, 'Here's the only money smarts you ever had.' That'll shut him up for once."

Opal smelled her flowers, then reached for the remote control box. "That Franklin, he always looks out for me. I guess you've seen this TV he gave me for Christmas."

"Yeah, it's great." I got up and edged toward the door. "I have to get back."

"He spoils me, and I love it." She mashed down on the button, and the channels began to shift.

I wandered over to Jack's place. He was leaning on a fender of the pickup, staring in at the humming engine. "Sounds pretty good," I said.

"I got off easy for once. It was just a little problem with the water pump. So I get to go study with Carol tonight after all."

"Carol? You're not going out with Julie on Valentine's Day?"

"We're going to a party tomorrow night."

I stood and looked at the engine for a minute. "I don't get it," I said finally. "If you're in love with Julie, how come you go out with other girls?"

Jack shrugged. "Variety. You can't just live on chocolate cake, even if it's your favorite."

"If Julie wanted to go out with you every night, would you turn her down?"

Jack laughed. "When that happens, I'll see."

"I just don't get you two. You used to go steady, and now you don't. But you still feel the same way about her, and I know she's in love with you."

"And you figure we ought to get married and live happily ever after, right?"

"I didn't say that."

"Look, it's not that easy. Julie keeps bringing me college catalogs and talking about careers. That's the senior blues, Eddie. Just when you start having fun, people want you to get serious about your life."

"What do you want to be—a junkman?"

"I can think of worse things." He reached into the truck and turned off the motor. "Sometimes I think I'd like to open a marine repair shop. There's not a decent one in this whole county. Guess what Julie thinks about that."

"I see what you mean." I shut the hood of the pickup. "You don't think things could change?"

Jack tossed a wrench in the direction of his toolbox. "Maybe in fifty years. Maybe Julie and I will be another pair like Opal and Pooch. We can sit around and watch the soaps together."

"I found out something about Pooch just now," I said. I leaned against the truck and told Jack about the woman from Lincoln Springs.

"Now we know why Pooch was so touchy," Jack said. "I knew it had to be something like that."

"Sure."

"You might as well learn to live with the facts, Eddie. You may not like 'em, but you can't change 'em. Mom dumped my old man out in the lake, and she found that license and bone under my bed. And Julie and I aren't going to get married. That's just the way things are."

"Happy Valentine's Day," I said, starting down the driveway. "If I ever need cheering up, I'll know where not to go."

Jack tossed a handful of gravel at me as I walked away. "Don't make a big deal out of it. That's just the facts."

I called out, "See you tomorrow," so that he'd know I wasn't mad, but I kept walking.

Coming up our driveway, I heard a yell. Ricky Batt was about a hundred feet up in an old Digger pine. "I see you," he yelled.

"I see you, too," I said. I wondered first how in the world he had gotten up there and then how he was going to get down again. I thought about telling somebody, then figured Ricky'd have a better chance if nobody got excited.

I would have gone on into the house, but Tony was standing at the bottom of the tree, crying his eyes out. "Hey, Tony," I said, "quit worrying. Ricky'll be all right."

Tony gave me a rotten look. "I want to go up there," he howled. "I want to go up there with Ricky."

I thought about what Opal had said and decided that I might be one of those bachelor types.

While I worked on my algebra that night, I came up with a plan. If Wayne Parks could have parties, why couldn't I? I decided on a Saturday picnic out on Pepperwood Island. With a little careful maneuvering, I could end up alone with Wendy.

I headed down to the docks to call her. I got the answering machine the first time, but a half hour later she answered.

"Hi, Eddie," she whispered. "Thank you for the flowers. They were beautiful."

"Let me guess," I said. "There's somebody around."

"They're in the living room, watching TV," she whispered. "Listen, I wanted to tell you. I gave the flowers to Miss Lennox. I hope that's okay."

The thought of my six-dollar flowers sitting on Miss Lennox's desk didn't exactly warm my heart, but I said, "Sure."

"I couldn't take them home, see? And I thought Miss Lennox would enjoy them." Then, in a normal voice, she said, "I still can't figure out problem five."

"I was thinking about having a party on Saturday," I said. "I thought maybe some people could come out to the marina, and we could go on a picnic out to Pepperwood Island."

"That sounds like fun." I could tell that somebody was still in the room. "Monday's a holiday, so we're going to Tahoe to go skiing for the three days."

So much for my plan. "I forgot about the holiday," I said. "I think I'll postpone the picnic for a week or two. I hope you can make it."

"Me too," she whispered. "Mom and Dad are a little tight about things like that."

I was disgusted walking back up the hill. I would have been in a worse mood if I had known then what I found out the next day: that Wayne Parks's family was also going to Tahoe for the weekend.

I was in my room working on my report when Julie got home. She had gone to dinner with Malcolm Hollingsworth, who was driving his father's Mercedes.

As usual, Mom was waiting up to hear the details. When I heard her go to bed, I wandered out to the kitchen.

"We went to Ricardo's in Carson Springs," Julie told me. "You should have seen it. Artichoke hearts, mushrooms stuffed with crab. Even caviar."

"I can do without the fish eggs," I said.

"It was incredible."

"What about Malcolm? Was he incredible too?"

"He's very nice," she said, sounding a little bored.

"I found out something today," I said. I told her about

Pooch's being married, finishing with "It's too bad. He was about the only suspect we had left."

Julie glared at me. "You just won't leave it alone, will you?"

"What's your problem?"

"Don't you see where you're heading? Who's left? Go ahead. Tell me who's left."

"Nobody."

"Don't give me that. I'll tell you who's left. Mom."

"Come on," I said. "Do you really think Mom dumped a body in the lake?"

"Maybe it wasn't that simple. You know what Mom's like—always trying to help somebody. Like the Batts. Anybody else would have chased them out long ago. Maybe somebody else was in trouble back then."

"You've been eating too many fish eggs," I said.

"All right, Mr. Detective, go get those shoeboxes." I went down the hall and got the boxes. She sat down at the kitchen table with them. "You went through all these. Did you notice anything?"

I pulled up a chair. "Like what?"

She began sorting through and laying out pictures. Not the kind I expected. The ones she put out were of boat trailers in the parking lot and of people backing down the boat ramp. And one of the restaurant after the new porch had been put on. "What do you make of all these?"

"I don't know what you're getting at," I said.

"Take another look." She hauled out a few of the early pictures and laid them in a row. "Do you notice a little difference?"

"So the place has been fixed up. I know that."

"Look at that retaining wall. Do you know how much something like that costs?"

"Will you just come out and say it?"

"You know the deal here. The resort has to pay for itself, right?"

Of course I knew that. We had heard it often enough. "So?"

"There's too much here," she said. "Now that we're bigger and fixed up better, we're taking in more money. But back when these things were put in, we just didn't make that much."

"Wait a minute," I said.

Julie hammered on the pictures with a finger. "Look at this and this and this. And this one. A lot of money was put into this place that didn't come out of the cash register."

"You really think—"

"No," she said quickly. "I don't think anything. And I'm not going to. As far as I'm concerned, everything's fine. I'm going to trust everybody. And you ought to do the same."

I figured that she wasn't really trusting anybody that way, but I couldn't think of a way to say it. I gathered up the pictures without saying any more.

"Listen," Julie said, "it's possible Mom had some money that we don't know about. There could be any number of explanations. But I figure there's a time to quit asking questions and just leave things alone."

"I agree."

She broke into a smile. "Really?"

"I'm finished."

"What about Jack?"

"You two ought to get together," I said. "He's sure *his* mother did it. The bag with the bone and stuff is missing, and Jack figures she took it."

"I'm glad that thing's gone," Julie said.

I put the pictures back into the boxes. "I think you're both wrong, but I'm through playing detective."

"Good."

"Happy Valentine's Day, Julie."

"Same to you." She grabbed my shoulders and gave me a hug. We both were a little awkward. We hadn't done much hugging in our lives.

14

I did my best to forget the whole thing, but whenever I saw the lake, I thought of the skeleton. And I kept looking at the parking lots and the retaining walls, almost checking for price tags.

Mom wasn't exactly the criminal type. She was a soft touch, who always ended up bringing refreshments and serving on the cleanup committee because she didn't have the heart to say no. Somebody was always asking her advice or crying on her shoulder. She took Opal shopping. She read stories to the Batt brats and taught them to count.

The only thing Mom wasn't softhearted about was the marina. When there were problems with the Forest Service or the restaurant suppliers, she was polite but tough as nails. The marina was her baby, and she would do anything to protect it. When she talked about the place, she got the same sparkle in her eye that she did when she was showing Julie's baby pictures or the sand painting I made in Cub Scouts.

I couldn't help wondering what Mom might do if she saw the marina in danger.

At the same time I couldn't picture Mom dumping a body in the lake under any circumstances.

I did nothing on my report over the long weekend. I just sat around getting depressed and wondering if anybody really knew what anybody else was like.

And when I really wanted to get into a blue funk, I'd picture Wendy and Wayne riding together on a chair lift up the mountain.

Things didn't get any better on Tuesday. Before I could say hello to Wendy, Wayne was pouring out stories about moguls and packed powder and snowball fights. I went into the algebra room early.

By that afternoon I had to talk to somebody. I went over to Jack's and found him working on the lanterns he had bought at the flea market. "I've fixed mine," he said. "How much will you pay me to fix yours?"

"I thought we were partners," I told him. "Fifty-fifty on everything."

Jack shoved a lantern into my hand. "Everything but the work. Take this thing apart."

"I've got something to tell you. Just don't make any comments until I'm done, all right?" While I dismantled the lantern, I told him about Mom and the improvements.

Jack worked beside me without saying a word.

"It's creepy," I said. "I want to forget the whole thing, but I can't. I'm almost afraid to talk around the house—afraid I might say something wrong."

"Now you know how I feel," Jack said. "Ever since

that bag disappeared, I've been walking on eggs. The only difference is, you're wrong." He took the lantern from me. "I'll take over here. You start on the next one."

"What makes you think I'm wrong?"

"It's impossible, that's why."

"She was here at the marina by herself. Dad and Julie and I were in San Diego."

"So what? Think about your mother, Eddie. She's just not the type. Whoever did this wanted to cover up something, and your mom isn't the cover-up type. No matter what happened, she'd just figure people could forgive and forget."

"Maybe so," I said.

"Don't get me wrong. She could do it if she had to. She's tough enough. But she wouldn't see any point in it."

"But where'd the money for the improvements come from?"

"I don't have an answer for that one," Jack said. "But no answer is better than a dumb one, like your mom ripping off a bank robber."

I wasn't completely satisfied, but I felt better. And we managed to fix all but one of the lanterns.

I thought about telling Julie what Jack had said. She had been moping around all weekend too. But I didn't have any real proof for her, and I wasn't sure she'd be happy about my telling Jack. So I let it go.

On my way to algebra on Wednesday morning I taped a pink envelope to the front of Wayne Parks's locker. The envelope was empty, but I hoped it would give me a minute or two alone with Wendy.

"Hey, Wayne," I said, coming up the hall, "who's sending you secret messages?"

Wayne glanced at Wendy, then said, "What do you mean?"

"Your locker's two-one-two, right? Well, there's a note on it. A pink one."

"Yeah, sure," Wayne said. "Probably from a skinny-dipper."

"Speaking of messages," Wendy said, "I'm supposed to give one to Eddie. You guys excuse us for a second." She led me away from the others.

"Who's the message from?" I asked.

Wendy turned toward me. "A secret admirer."

"Oh, yeah?"

"Here's the message: I wish I could have gone on the picnic last Saturday."

"Me too." I glanced back at Wayne.

"Wayne's a good guy," Wendy said, "and his parents and mine are good friends, but he's like a brother to me."

I leaned against the wall with a Popsicle-licking grin on my face. It wasn't me playing the pesty Arthur Prentice role after all; it was Wayne. "You want to go on a picnic this weekend?" I asked.

"I'd like to, but I don't think my parents would let me."

"How about the basketball tournament Friday night?"

"I can probably meet you there."

Miss Lennox stepped into the hallway and said, "Let's go now."

"Great," I told Wendy. "I'll call you tonight."

"It might be better if you didn't."

"Maybe I could call up and say it was a wrong number, just to let you know I was thinking about you."

She reached over and squeezed my arm. "I'll know anyway."

Heading into the room, I watched Wayne Parks go tromping down the hall. I felt a little sorry for him.

After school that day Jack and I headed for the docks to check out the fishing. "You and I'd better go out on the lake Saturday," he said. "It's time for us to get back to the important things in life."

I gave him the latest about Wendy, finishing with "I'd rather go on a picnic, but seeing her at the tournament is better than nothing."

Jack laughed. "The old better-than-nothing business again. Another verse of the freshman blues."

"I'm not singing the blues," I said.

"With parents like hers around, you will be soon enough."

We stopped by the blackboard and saw that the fishing had been upgraded to "good." Woody had recommended minnows for bait and chalked in "Browns around Pepperwood Island."

"Let's add a note," Jack said. "Skeletons by Prentice Point."

"Quiet," I said, glancing over at the store. Sure enough, Pooch was standing right in the doorway.

"Don't believe everything you read, boys," he said.

"I was around Pepperwood this morning, and nobody was catching a thing."

"Nice going, Jack," I muttered.

"Come here and look at this," Pooch whispered, holding out a dime.

"What about it?" I asked.

"I got it at the coin shop in town. Paid three bucks for it. Just watch old Woodrow have kittens."

We followed Pooch inside. Woody was moving down the aisle, straightening the cans.

Pooch took a Hershey bar from the rack and handed Woody a dollar bill. "Here you go, Woodrow."

Woody slipped the dollar into the register and set Pooch's change on the counter.

Pooch grabbed the coins and stepped back. "Funny-looking dime, Woodrow." He held it in front of me. "Can you read the date on that, Eddie?"

"It's 1937," I said.

Woody reached out his hand. "Give me that thing."

Pooch backed away. "Not so fast, Woodrow. You gave it out to me, so it's mine now."

"It was a mistake," Woody said. "Give it to me." He grabbed another dime from the register. "Here. I'll trade you."

Pooch held up his dime. "No, thanks. I believe I'll keep this one."

"It's mine," Woody said. "I gave it to you by accident."

Pooch stripped the wrapper off his candy. "Well, that's the breaks, Woodrow. You'll have to be more careful next time." He took a bite of candy and flipped the coin into the air. "Heads or tails?" He caught the coin and flipped it again. "Call it, and it's yours, Woodrow." He gave the coin another flip.

"Tails," Woody said.

Pooch caught the coin and slapped it onto the back of his other hand. "It's heads. Too bad." He scooped up the coin before anybody had a chance to look at it.

"It was an accident," Woody said. "Give it to me."

"You sure, Woodrow? You absolutely sure this is yours?"

"Yes."

Pooch took another bite of candy. "Positive?"

"Yes."

Pooch held up the dime. "That's funny. It looks exactly like the one I bought yesterday at the coin shop."

"Get out!" Woody yelled.

Pooch began to howl. "You should have seen your face, Woodrow."

"Out!"

"Now, Woodrow, don't be a bad sport."

"And don't come back," Woody yelled.

Pooch kept grinning, but he moved toward the door. "You'd better be careful. I may be forced to take my business somewhere else."

"You're finished here," Woody said.

Pooch stopped in the doorway and flipped the dime toward the counter. "Since you're positive this is yours, you'd better take it." He laughed and banged the door shut.

Woody picked up the dime and stuck it in his pocket. "Stupid old fool," he muttered. He locked the register and stomped out.

"How long do you figure this one will last?" I asked Jack.

"Not more'n a day or two. Woody got the dime, so he won't stay mad too long."

"You know—" I started.

"That's it!" Jack burst out. "That's the answer."

"What?"

"Who got Woody started collecting coins?" Jack said.

"My grandpa. You know that." And then it hit me too. "Oh, I see what—"

"He collected coins for years and years, right? And where'd they all go?"

"Mom got them, but—"

"Well, there's your answer. When she needed money for the place, she sold them."

"But she didn't," I said.

"Are you sure?"

"Look, Mom was still putting in coins last fall. So the collection is still in the safe where it always was." My grandfather had built a hidden safe into the floor of our house. It was a secret, and Jack was probably the only one outside our family who knew about it.

"Maybe," Jack said.

After that I *had* to check the safe. Jack and I came up with a couple of plans to get everybody out of my house, but we ended up not needing them. The next day Mom met Julie after school to go shopping and left us a clear field.

The safe was below the floor of my parents' bedroom, under the bed. I moved the rug back, lifted out a square of floorboards, and turned the dial. I wasn't supposed to know the combination, but I had known it for five years.

Nothing inside looked any different from the last time I had opened it six months before. There were a couple of rings and a bracelet that had belonged to my grandmother and a few legal papers. The rest of the box —the reason the safe had been built—was taken up by the bulky blue pages of the coin folders.

I lifted out one batch of the pages and scooted backward. I sat on the bedroom floor and flipped through sheets of nickels. I felt like throwing them against the wall. "See?" I said to Jack. "I told you the stuff was still here. But you didn't believe me."

"It was a good idea, though." He thumbed through some pages. "Look at all this money. What do you figure these things are worth?"

"Who cares?"

"I was just wondering. What do you figure?"

"Some of them are only worth fifty cents or so. I guess some of the older ones might be worth twenty or thirty bucks."

"Not any more than that?"

"A few, I guess. Grandpa bought some uncirculated ones. Come on, don't mess things up."

Jack turned to another page. "This is neat. Looking at all this money could get to you, though. I start wanting all of it."

I began to stack the pages. "We'd better put things away."

"Just a minute," Jack said. "I've always heard about Indian head pennies, but these are the first ones I've seen." He turned over another page. "This is really messed up." He flipped to another. "This one too."

"What are you talking about?"

"The folder says '1915,' but there's a 1968 in it. And here's a 1972."

I checked his page, then grabbed another out of the middle. I turned to another page, then another, and another. "You're right," I said, and broke out laughing.

Jack looked over at me. "You mean?"

"Yep. These aren't messed up. Mom just sold off a lot of the good ones. But to keep anybody from realizing it, she put other coins in their place."

"Why bother? I mean, they belonged to her, didn't they?"

But I understood it. Dad would never have stood for Mom's cashing in the coins to fix up the marina. So she did it secretly. She knew he'd never do more than glance at the folders anyway.

Jack gave me a shove. "I knew your mom didn't have anything to do with that bank money."

I slid under the bed and carefully packed the pages back into the safe. When everything was in place, Jack and I went out to the kitchen and dug into the cookie jar. Suddenly I was starving.

15

When Julie got home that afternoon, I got her aside and told her about the coins. "Well," she said, "I knew it had to be something like that. I mean, let's be serious." But she looked awfully relieved.

A few minutes later she came into my room and wanted to hear every last detail. "Wow," she said, "I feel better. I mean, I know it was dumb, but once you start thinking about that kind of thing, everything gets crazy. I was actually watching Mom, expecting maybe to see something that might give her away. I mean, how stupid is that?"

"I was just as bad," I told her.

"Listen, Eddie, next time you two drag something dirty out of the lake, throw it back. Fast."

While we were eating dinner, Barbara Batt came to the door and told Mom that some museum people were interested in Roger's sculpture. "They can only pay two thousand. That isn't as much as Roger wants, but he may let it go."

"He'd better grab the money and run," Dad muttered.

After Barbara had left, Mom came dancing back to the table. "Isn't that wonderful?"

"Yes," Dad said. "Now maybe they'll be able to afford a new place."

I wondered what the museum people saw when they looked at that pile of rusty metal. I also wondered how Roger was going to get it out of the cabin. It was already too big to fit through the door.

After dinner I got out the shoeboxes, but I was feeling too good to bury myself in homework. I started looking at some of the family pictures that I had set aside—ones of Dad while he still had all his hair and some choice ones of Julie with braids and missing teeth.

I flipped through snapshots of me in a crib and on a tricycle and riding on Grandpa's shoulders. It was hard to believe that the funny-looking kid was really me.

I stopped to examine a picture of me beside a birthday cake with a big "5" on it. I was holding a fire engine with both hands, as if it were about to fly away. I remembered that fire engine. I had spotted it in the Western Auto store during the summer and decided right then that I had to have it for Christmas. I reminded Mom and Dad several times a day. I must have driven them crazy. Instead of waiting until Christmas, they gave it to me for my birthday (November 7) instead.

The next picture was one of our family by the Christmas tree. Julie was holding her arm out in front of her to show off her new watch. I had some presents in front of me, but in my hand was my fire engine. It was bent like a boomerang.

Then I remembered that my fire engine had been run over. Grandpa had pounded it out as well as he could. Then he had said for me to pretend it was turning a corner.

As I sat there with the shoebox in my lap, the whole thing came back to me, and I was furious all over again. I had been playing outside when Mom called me for lunch. I had left my fire engine where it was, about five feet from the edge of the driveway. Then, while we were eating, we had heard a crunch. Jack's father had run over my fire engine. I don't know why he had swerved that far, but he had. He stopped his car in front of our house, went back and picked up the fire engine, and claimed it had been in the driveway.

Of course, because he was a grown-up, everybody believed him and thought I had been taught a valuable lesson. I tried to show everybody where the fire engine had been, but nobody would listen. And I was finally sent to my room because I wouldn't shut up about it.

A tear fell onto the picture I was holding.

Mom glanced into my room as she walked past. "What's the matter, Eddie?"

"Nothing."

She came inside and looked down at the pictures. "Are you thinking about Grandpa?" She reached down and squeezed my shoulder. "I miss him too."

"Mom," I burst out, "he lied."

"Grandpa?"

"No. Jack's father."

Mom laughed and shook her head. "What in the world are you talking about?"

"Do you remember when Mr. Mason ran over my fire engine?"

"No."

"He said it was in the driveway, but it wasn't. He lied about that, and then everybody believed him. And I got sent to my room and scolded for lying. And I *didn't.* It was him. He lied, and everybody believed him." I was so mad that I started sobbing like a little kid. "Do you remember?"

"No," Mom said, "I don't remember it at all." She rubbed the back of my neck. "But I believe you. And I'm sorry I didn't believe you then."

"It was the meanest thing anybody ever did to me."

"I'm sorry," Mom whispered.

"He was a real rat." I glanced down at the picture of me standing by the birthday cake. "I'm telling you, if I ever have a kid and he tells me something, I'm going to believe it."

Mom smiled. "That's a good idea. He'll probably be lying ninety percent of the time, but you'd better believe it anyway. Because sometimes he'll be telling the truth."

"Come on," I said. "I didn't lie."

"You were terrible," Mom said. "I'd catch you with a mouthful of cookies and one in your hand, and you'd swear you hadn't been near the cookie jar."

I started to laugh. "I don't remember anything like that."

Mom smiled. "I'm not surprised."

"But I remember about the fire engine," I said, "and that time I was telling the truth."

Then it struck me. It probably would have hit me before if I hadn't been so caught up in my memories. I grabbed the pictures and headed for the door. "I have to see Jack," I said over my shoulder.

"Get your jacket," Mom said, but I didn't bother.

I ran all the way. The light was on in Jack's bedroom, so I headed straight for the side door.

"Hey, Jack," I yelled.

"Come on in, Eddie." He was lying on his bed, surrounded by schoolbooks and magazines.

"Look at these." I kicked some coveralls aside, stepped over a stack of cassettes, and handed him the two snapshots. Then I pushed aside a pile of *Popular Mechanics* magazines and collapsed on the corner of the bed.

"You're puffing like a steam engine," Jack said.

"Look at those."

He studied the pictures. "I don't know what happened to you, Eddie. You used to be a good-looking little kid."

"I got that fire engine on my fifth birthday," I said between breaths. "November seventh. Ten days after that bank was robbed. And your father ran over it. See the Christmas picture? See how it's bent?"

Jack looked at the pictures, then tossed them toward me. "What is this, Eddie?"

"It's proof, you moron. Your dad was still around here after November seventh. He ran over my truck and lied about it. I just remembered it when I saw these pictures."

"Sort of convenient," Jack said. "You just happened to see these today, huh?"

"Cut that out," I told him. "This is the truth. He was a dirty, rotten slimeball. I don't care if he *was* your father. He lied and got me in trouble—a little five-year-old kid. But he was alive then anyway."

Jack reached for the pictures. "Give it to me again. Slower."

I told him the whole story. My throat got tight when I talked about being sent to my room.

"You're still mad about it, aren't you?" Jack said.

"Darn right. It was bad enough that he ran over my fire engine, but then he got me into trouble besides."

"That's good old Daddy for you," Jack said. "You're sure about the time?"

"Check the cake. That's my fifth birthday."

Jack handed me the pictures, then laughed, and jabbed me with his foot. "Detective Eddie. You just keep going, don't you?"

"This one was pure accident," I said.

"You can work on my case anytime, buddy." He took a long breath and blew it out. "Oh, man, all of a sudden I feel a lot better."

"This has been a good day," I said.

Jack flopped back on the bed for a minute or two, his head resting on his physics book. Then he sat up and looked at me. "Sort of changes things around, doesn't it?"

"Not for me. I told you a long time ago your theory about your mom was a bunch of garbage."

He grinned. "I guess you did." He lay back again "So, Detective Eddie, how do you figure it?"

"I don't. We're out of suspects."

He nudged me with his foot. "You can do better than that."

"We've already had two big discoveries today. What do you expect?"

"You know, if Daddy wasn't the one being dumped in the lake, then *he* could have done the dumping."

"Maybe," I said, "but I'll bet he didn't come back and steal the license plate out of here the other night."

Jack shook his head. "That's the part I can't figure. It doesn't make any sense. It never did. Think about it. Back when it happened, why did somebody bother taking that license plate? The car was right there, registered to August Bartolozzi. And August's body was right there too. What was the point of taking the license?" He looked around the room. "And then it disappears from here."

I glanced down at the mounds of clothes and magazines on his floor. "You sure it didn't just get buried?"

"Come on."

"I'm serious. A guy could lose an elephant in here."

Jack waved me away. "There's got to be some kind of explanation." He slid off the bed and headed for the door, weaving between the piles. "Mom," he yelled from the hallway, "have you been in my room lately?"

"Are you kidding?" she called back. "I'd be afraid of getting typhoid."

"I can't find some stuff. I thought maybe you did some housecleaning."

"No chance. I wouldn't go into your room on a bet. I hold my breath when I walk by the door."

Jack came back through the door and used his foot to clear a path to the bed. "Nothing's ever easy."

When I headed for home, Jack came along with me. He went on and on about how stupid he had been. "It was bad enough before," he said, "but ever since that bag disappeared, I've been a basket case. I was sure Mom was hiding all these big secrets, but she kept acting the same as always. So I figured she was *really* a tough one."

"That's the trouble with playing detective," I said. "Pretty soon you don't believe anybody." We were passing Woody and Opal's mailbox. I could hear the noise from their TV set.

"That license plate still bothers me," Jack said. "Why would somebody—" He dropped to one knee. "Hold it. My shoe's untied."

"Maybe it—" I started.

"Talk about school," Jack whispered.

"What?"

"Somebody's behind those trees. Talk about school."

I started rattling on about my geography class. I couldn't see anything out there.

Jack stood up, and we walked on toward our mailbox. I kept spouting some nonsense about the kind of tests Mr. Crowell gave while Jack looked over his shoulder.

We stopped at the mailbox. "Somebody's back there," Jack muttered.

"What'll we do?"

"I'll jog back toward my place. You start up the driveway and hide. One of us should get a look at him." He called out, "See you tomorrow, Eddie," and ran off.

I said, "See ya," and walked toward our house. Halfway there I ducked behind a big pine and waited. The only sounds I could hear came from Opal's TV.

Then I saw a figure move past our mailbox. I tiptoed forward. As the figure walked under the light by the restaurant, I spotted the silver hair. Pooch.

I ran down the driveway. "Hey, Pooch," I yelled.

He spun around, throwing his hands in the air. When he spotted me, he muttered something I didn't catch.

"What's happening?" I asked.

"You scared the pie out of me," he said. "I didn't know anybody was around."

"What are you doing?"

"Not much."

I stood and waited, but he didn't say any more. "You been to Woody's?"

"Nope."

I said, "What?" before I thought, but he didn't seem to hear.

"Woodrow's still mad about that dime. Wouldn't even look at me today." He chuckled, then asked, "What are you up to?"

"I was just over at Jack's place."

He stretched out his arms and yawned. "I think I'll have a little swim and go to bed." He headed down the hill. "Good night, Eddie."

Jack was waiting for me by our mailbox. "He said he hadn't been to Woody's."

"I heard him."

"He *must* have been there."

"Let's go find out," Jack said.

We planned to knock on Woody's door and pretend to be looking for Pooch, but the door opened just as we reached the porch. Opal stepped outside and picked up a paper bag.

"Hi, Opal," I said.

She smiled at us. "Hello, Eddie. Hello, Jack." She held out the bag. "That goofy Pooch. He just called up and said he left something on the porch for me." She opened the bag and looked inside. "Brownies. You want some?" Jack and I each took one. "Pooch uses a box mix—add some water and stir—and then thinks he's the big chef." She laughed and popped a brownie into her mouth.

"They're pretty good," I said.

"They're okay for a box mix," she said, still chewing. "When I get to feeling better, I'll make you some of the real ones, and you can see the difference."

"Anytime you need a brownie tester, just whistle," Jack said. "We'll come running."

"You boys looking for Woody?" Opal asked.

"Actually," I said, "we were looking for Pooch."

"He's back at the docks. That's where he just called from." She laughed and took another brownie. "The big chef." She moved back inside. "I'd better get back to my program. I guess you've seen the TV that my boy Franklin sent me."

"What do you think?" I asked Jack once we were away from the house.

"I think that was the worst brownie I've had in a long time," he said.

16

When I came outside with my books and my lunch the next morning, Jack was in the parking lot, talking to the Batt brats.

"What's the matter?" I asked when he came back toward the truck. "Have they been throwing rocks again?"

"Talking a little business," Jack said. "I figured that if there was anything missing around here, Ricky and Tony were the first ones to ask."

"You think they might have taken the bag out of your room?"

"Why not? I told them I'd trade them a Milky Way for the license if they had it for me this afternoon."

I looked toward the empty parking lot. "What did they say?"

"As soon as they heard about the Milky Way, they took off like a shot."

Jack climbed into the pickup. I opened the door on the passenger side and said, "Hey, Jack, can I get a ride to the basketball tournament tonight? Mom and Dad have to go to a Chamber of Commerce dinner."

"How would you like me to come along on *your* dates?"

"Give me a break. I'm supposed to meet Wendy there. Five bucks for gas money, all right?"

"Your love life's interfering with mine."

"But you wouldn't turn down your pal Detective Eddie, would you?"

Jack started to laugh, and I knew it was settled. I also knew he'd remember about the five dollars.

That afternoon Jack and I went down to the docks and bought a couple of Milky Way bars. Pooch put down his sugar sacks long enough to put the money in the cash register.

"You and Woody must be friends again," I said.

Pooch grinned. "I wouldn't say friends exactly."

"If he left you with the money, he can't be too mad," Jack said.

"Yeah, but he counted all of it beforehand—with me sitting right here. He was just hoping I'd say something." Pooch ran his fingers through his hair. "I think Opal's giving Woodrow a hard time these days. He won't fight back, of course. Afraid she'll have a heart attack on the spot. So he stores it all up, then comes down here and takes it out on me."

"And, of course, you never fight back," I said.

Pooch laughed. "A good fight's healthy. Gets your blood pumping."

The Batt brats were waiting for us at the end of the walkway. Ricky had a big paper bag in his hand.

"Whatcha got?" Jack asked him.

"Something."

Jack waved a Milky Way bar in front of him. "Let's see."

Ricky held the bag behind his back and reached for the candy with his other hand.

"Hold it," Jack said. "This is a trade. Do you have a license plate in there?" Ricky nodded. "Give me the bag, and I'll give you the candy bar."

Ricky shook his head. "Uhh-uhh."

"Why not?"

"We get five Milky Ways."

"Five?"

Ricky's head bobbed up and down. "We got five licenses."

"Wonderful," I said.

"Two Milky Ways for the whole bag," Jack told him. "And that's my final offer." He waved the candy bars in front of Ricky. Tony inched closer, reaching out his hand.

Ricky dropped the bag, grabbed the two candy bars, and went racing up the hill with Tony right behind him.

I turned the bag upside down. License plates clattered onto the ground. I pawed through them, but August Bartolozzi's wasn't there. "Mom's counting lessons aren't working very well," I said. "There are six plates here."

Jack snorted. "That's three apiece, but you can have my share."

We decided to tack the plates onto the bulletin board outside the store and hope the owners found them. One of the plates had a circled *E,* which meant it came off a government vehicle—probably Vince Minetti's patrol car.

On our way back up the hill, we noticed that Woody's pickup was missing a rear plate. "One of us ought to put his license back on," Jack said.

"I wonder which one."

"Probably the one who needs a favor tonight." He leaned against the truck while I went back across the walkway and got the plate. I even bought some bolts at the store.

Jack watched me put on the plate. "This business with the Batt brats was one of my stupidest ideas yet," he said. "Even if those two had gotten into my room, they never would have found that bag. Too many other good things to steal right out in the open."

I tightened the last bolt. "I guess."

"I hadn't thought it through before now. Up until last night I thought Mom had found it. Who else would go digging under my bed?"

I looked up at him, ready to answer that question. But he was already grinning.

Things were quiet in the pickup as we drove to the tournament. Julie had been moping around all afternoon. If Los Cedros lost the game, basketball season was over. And so was her career as a cheerleader.

She looked down at her blue and gold sweater, sighed, and said, "I may never wear this outfit again."

"That's real confidence," I told her. "If we win tonight, there's another game tomorrow, and if we win that, we play on Monday night."

"They beat us by thirty points last month," she said. "And their best player was hurt."

"Boy, you know how to get our hopes up, don't you?"

"I just hope it's close," she said. "Our last game—I hope everybody doesn't end up leaving early."

"Enough about basketball," Jack broke in. "I've got something to say."

"I know what it is," I said. "You decided it wouldn't be fair to charge me five dollars to go watch a slaughter."

"Shut up, Eddie. I'm serious for a change." He let that sink in, then went on. "A couple of weeks ago, when we found those stories in the library, I gave you two a hard time. I knew all the answers and wouldn't listen to anybody. I was being really stupid, and I'm sorry about it."

"We were all stupid," Julie said.

"All my life I've known that my father was a jerk," Jack went on, "but it still bothered me to find out he was dead."

Julie reached up and put her arm around his shoulders. "It's been hard."

"I had these crazy ideas about my mom. First she was a murderer. Then she dumped my dad in the lake. I was afraid she'd be put in jail."

Julie patted the back of his neck. "That's awful."

"And then Eddie showed me I was wrong."

Julie looked my way. "Eddie?"

"That's right. Good old Detective Eddie."

"Why didn't you tell me?" she said.

"I just figured it out last night." I gave her a quick version of the fire engine story.

"So I was wrong," Jack said when I finished. "But it got me thinking about how far I would have gone to keep my mother from getting into trouble. If I saw some way to protect her, wouldn't I take it? What if I had a chance to get rid of the only proof against her? I'd be crazy not to do it."

"You're talking about me, aren't you?" Julie whispered.

I couldn't hold back any longer. "You took the bag from under Jack's bed, didn't you?"

Julie nodded. "Yes."

"It had to be you," Jack said. "You were the only one who knew it was there."

Julie slid down in the seat. "Crazy, crazy, crazy. Once I got hold of the idea that Mom was part of it, I quit thinking straight. Mom wouldn't have—"

"What did you do with the stuff?" I asked her.

"I threw it back into the lake."

"Good," Jack said.

"When?" I asked.

"Valentine's night. You remember that big purse I was carrying? I had Malcolm stop in the middle of the bridge—right where Jack told us that day. And I had a rock in the bag to make sure it would sink."

"But—" I started.

"Don't worry," she said. "Malcolm thought they were old letters."

"Best place in the world for that stuff," Jack said. "Two hundred feet underwater, even in a drought year."

"I wanted to tell you today, but I was afraid to," she said, wrapping herself around him.

While the two of them snuggled and whispered, I stared out the window and thought about Julie's trying to protect Mom. A minute later the whole murky problem came clear: I knew what had happened nine years before.

I didn't even consider saying anything right then. After all my exploded theories in the past weeks, I wanted to consider all the angles before shooting off my mouth.

Besides, Jack and Julie had other things on their minds.

The high school gym was packed to the rafters. I spent half an hour looking for Wendy before locating her in the mob at the far doorway. Her father was right behind her.

"Hello, Mr. Westfall," I said.

"Hello, Willy."

"Daddy," Wendy said, "it's Eddie."

The three of us stood in the crowded doorway for the entire first half, packed together so closely that I couldn't move my foot without stepping on one of theirs. By halftime Los Cedros was trailing by twenty-five points, and Mr. Westfall had had enough. Wendy tried to work on him, but he was finished. "Good-bye, Willy," he said.

I watched them walk away. Wendy looked back and waved. Right then I decided it was time to quit standing around. I dashed forward, weaving through the crowd.

Mr. Westfall looked surprised to see me walking beside them, but he didn't say anything until we reached the sidewalk. Then he stopped, looked my way, and said, "Well, good night."

"I'll walk to your car with you," I said.

Wendy looked worried, but I just smiled and stayed with them.

When we got to their car, Mr. Westfall hauled out his keys and opened the door on the passenger side.

Wendy slid into the seat. "Good night, Eddie."

"Good night," I said.

Her father slammed the door and started around the car.

"Excuse me, Mr. Westfall," I called out. He gave me the kind of look most people save for things they find squashed in the road. "Would you mind if I rode my bicycle over to your house on Sunday afternoon?"

That caught him off guard. For a minute he didn't say anything. Then he began with "Well, I'm not sure what—"

"I won't be any trouble," I said. "I'm kind of funny-looking, but I'm a pretty good guy. You can ask my mother."

Mr. Westfall actually laughed. "Yeah. Come on over."

"Thank you, sir," I told him. "I'll see you Sunday."

The night went downhill fast from there. Los Cedros lost by forty points, Julie cried most of the way home, and Jack didn't forget to stop at the gas station.

But I still went to bed with a smile on my face.

17

I woke up at two-thirty and couldn't go back to sleep. I was sure I knew what had happened nine years ago, but it wasn't enough just to know. I wanted to get everything settled once and for all.

At four o'clock I came up with a plan. I spent fifteen minutes writing a message in my English notebook and another five copying that message in block letters on a fresh piece of paper. Then I delivered the message before I changed my mind. Afterward I crawled back into my warm bed, glad to be finished. But I still couldn't sleep.

While Dad and I were eating breakfast, Jack stopped by on his way to the flea market. Jack wanted some company, but Dad had a father-son morning planned—weeding the flower beds. While we crawled between the rosebushes, Dad and I talked about the San Francisco Giants, who were about to start spring training. In the middle of a discussion of split-fingered fastballs, I found myself wondering if Dad had any secrets buried in his past. That's what detective work does to you.

After lunch Jack was back with his fishing rod and tackle box. "How'd we do at the flea market?" I asked him.

"Not bad. You made twenty-six bucks, and I made thirty-five."

"I thought we were partners."

"My lanterns sold for more money than yours did."

The fishing blackboard outside the store said the recommended bait was minnows. Jack and I never used minnows. It seemed unfair to use fish to catch fish. But if minnows were working, we'd try silver lures.

"Any action today?" Jack asked Woody.

Woody pulled on his hatbrim and shrugged. "Here and there."

"How would Woodrow know?" Pooch broke in. "He's been here in the store all day. I was out all morning. Caught a big mess of bass by the Pine Creek inlet."

Woody snorted. "He brought home one little fish."

"No use keeping more than I can eat."

Woody snorted again.

"Hear that?" Pooch said. "Woodrow must be coming down with a cold. Doesn't have any hair to keep his head warm."

Jack and I loaded our gear into the old aluminum boat. I handled the motor while he stretched out in front. The red scar between the waterline and the trees had shrunk, but we still needed more rain.

"So how's your love life?" Jack yelled over his shoulder.

"Not too bad. I'm going to ride my bike over to Wendy's house tomorrow."

"Your bike? How far is it?"

"About fifteen miles. Of course, if I could find a buddy with a pickup, he could take me and the bike over that way."

"I hope you find one. Things go okay last night?"

"It was a bomb. It cost me five dollars to stand next to her father for an hour."

"It's another verse of the freshman blues," Jack said. "You know what'll happen tomorrow, don't you? You'll ride all that way, and then her father won't let you out of his sight."

"At least I'll get to talk to Wendy for a while without Wayne Parks around."

"Oh, you'll have a great talk. You and her dad and her mother and her sisters."

I scooped a handful of water from the bottom of the boat and threw it at him.

"You know what you'd do if you were smart, Eddie? You'd save Wendy for a couple of years. She's cute now, but she'll be even cuter in a year or two. You'll have a car then, and she'll be able to go out."

"And what am I supposed to do in the meantime?"

"I know just the girl to help you pass the time—Marjorie Stanton."

"I don't even know her."

"She's a junior. Her dad just gave her a new Toyota Celica for her sixteenth birthday. Get the picture? No transportation problems. No hassles with meeting her parents. It's perfect."

"She's too old for me."

"No way. She's sixteen, but she acts twelve. You two'll get along fine."

"You're a real buddy."

Jack laughed. "You're too fussy, Ed. Freshmen can't afford to be fussy."

While we headed across open water, I spotted a couple of boats trolling in the coves and another anchored off a rocky point. I was beginning to have second thoughts about the message I had delivered that morning. I had to tell Jack about it, but first I wanted to get as close as possible to Prentice Point.

When we roared past Pepperwood Island, Jack pointed that way and yelled, "Let's give it a shot."

"Let's go on."

"I've got a feeling," Jack yelled. "Cut over there."

I had put things off as long as I could. I cut back on the throttle and flipped the engine out of gear.

Jack turned back toward me. "What's the matter?"

I handed him my copy of the message. "Read this."

"What is it?"

"Just read it."

Jack glanced at the first line, then looked up at me. "What are you up to?" Then he went back to the paper.

At four o'clock in the morning the note had seemed perfect. Three simple sentences: "I KNOW ALL ABOUT THE OCTOBER 27 BANK ROBBERY IN SAN FRANCISCO WHERE AUGUST BARTOLOZZI WAS KILLED. AT 3:30 SATURDAY AFTERNOON, COME TO THE SPOT WHERE YOU LEFT AUGUST'S PARTNER, AND THE WHOLE THING CAN BE CLEARED UP. I WILL NOT MAKE TROUBLE FOR YOU." Watching Jack read it, I kept thinking of other things I could have put down.

Jack handed me the paper and said, "Don't send it."

"Why not?"

He grabbed the front of my shirt. "You already sent it, didn't you?"

"I had to know," I said.

Jack shoved me backward, letting go of my shirt. "And you didn't figure we ought to talk it over first?"

"It just hit me last night. It was like an algebra problem. I just happened to look at things in a different way, and suddenly everything fell into place." Jack looked out across the water. "Come on, Jack. Don't be mad. I would have told you. But it was the middle of the night, and I just wanted to get the whole thing over with. So I wrote that note and delivered it."

"Wonderful."

"All right. I shouldn't have done it that way. But I was sick and tired of it all. Once I figured out what happened, I couldn't wait to get the whole thing behind us."

Jack looked back at me. "Let's hear it. Right now."

"Promise me one thing first."

"What?"

"Promise you'll go over to Prentice Point with me, even if you don't believe me."

Jack hauled himself to his feet, and the boat rocked crazily. "Who did it? If you don't tell me right now, you're going over the side."

So I told him.

He sat down slowly. "Are you sure?"

"We'll find out soon enough." I put the engine in gear and twisted the throttle.

When we were almost to Prentice Point, Jack waved for me to slow down. "We're early. We might as well troll a little."

I wasn't very interested in fishing right then, but I was ready to do whatever Jack said—as long as he didn't want to go home. I put on a Thin Fin, tossed it into the water, and let out about thirty yards of line.

While we chugged along, I kept running back over everything we had learned. At four in the morning all the answers had been clear. Now my mind started coming up with other possibilities.

"There you go!" Jack yelled.

I looked up to see my rod bending. By the time I woke up enough to set my hook, the fish was gone. I waved the empty rod. "Nobody home."

"That's all right," Jack said. "Leave some for the tourists."

I watched Prentice Point get bigger and bigger as we plowed through the calm water. I wondered what to do if somebody was already in the cove. I was glad to have Jack there, stretched out in the front of the boat.

The cove was empty. Just to make sure, I made a wide loop before beaching the boat. "What time is it?" I asked Jack.

"Still too early."

I expected Jack to ask some questions, but he didn't. I wondered whether he believed me, but I wasn't about to ask.

We killed time casting from shore and slowly retrieving our lures. I didn't expect to catch anything that way, but that kind of fishing keeps you busy at least. Right away Jack caught a perch that wasn't much bigger than his lure. "Here's your dinner, Eddie."

"Maybe you could use him for bait," I said.

Far in the distance a motor was buzzing. I set my rod aside and kept my eyes on the opening to the cove. A white fishing boat passed by at trolling speed. "What time is it?" I asked again.

In the next half hour Jack and I each caught and released two small bass. It's possible that we caught the same fish four times. I wasn't paying that much attention to details.

I looked around at the empty lake and the bare shoreline. I wouldn't have minded a boatload of fishermen across the way—just in case I hadn't figured things exactly right. I didn't think we were in danger, but I had been wrong a good many times in the past weeks.

"Hear that?" Jack said. "Somebody's coming."

I heard the low hum of a motor for half a minute before the boat appeared in the opening to the cove. It was a white, low-slung boat, moving past at trolling speed. At that distance I couldn't be sure how many people were in it.

When the boat was almost to the far side of the opening, I cast out my lure again. "False alarm."

Just as my lure hit the water, the boat made a slow turn to the right and headed into the cove, following the opposite bank. I reeled in my line without taking my eyes off the boat.

The boat crawled along, staying about thirty feet away from the opposite shoreline. A single person was hunched down in the back. Long before I could make out the face, I recognized the straw hat.

"It's Woody," Jack said. "You were right."

The boat continued along the far bank until it was straight across from us. By then I had recognized it as number seventeen from our rental boats, a white fiberglass job.

Woody reeled in his line, then steered the boat across the water toward us. When he was about forty feet in front of us, he turned the boat sideways and flipped the motor out of gear. "Any luck?"

"Nothing worth keeping," Jack said. "What about you?"

"Just got started." Woody looked toward Prentice Point, then back at us. "You boys might try out around Pepperwood Island. This morning a guy said—"

"It's okay, Woody," I called out. "I sent the note."

"What?" Woody glared at me.

"I put it on the steering wheel of your pickup this morning."

Woody shook his head and turned away. He put his outboard motor into gear and brought his boat to shore beside ours. He shut off the motor and threw his fishing pole aside before he looked at me again. "You were the one?" he shouted.

I nodded. I hadn't expected him to be angry.

Woody stepped from his boat onto the bank, yanked the boat halfway out of the water, then turned to face me. "What did you do it for?"

I moved backward, trying to think of a way to answer.

"Take it easy, Woody," Jack said.

Woody started toward me. "I'm talking to Eddie."

Jack stepped into Woody's path. "What did you want him to do—call the cops, call the newspaper?"

Woody tried to move around Jack, but Jack stayed in his way.

"Settle down and think about it," Jack said. "We found a skeleton out here, tied to a motor from the marina. We kept it secret because we didn't want to make trouble for anybody. You ought to be thanking us, not getting mad."

Woody thought about that for a minute before he muttered, "I about fainted when I saw that note."

"Let's just sit down a minute," Jack said. Woody glared in my direction. "Eddie's sorry he scared you. He was just trying to get things straightened out without making any trouble." Jack turned toward me. "Apologize, Eddie."

"I'm sorry, Woody," I said.

Woody waved me away and plopped down onto the wet ground. Jack dropped to one knee. I came over and sat beside Jack.

"That note knocked me for a loop," Woody said, looking toward the lake. "I hadn't thought about any of this for years. Didn't really forget, but I did, in a way."

Jack told him about finding the bones and the license plate.

"I never thought about the lake getting that low," Woody said.

"And you had no idea we'd found anything?" Jack asked him. "Not even when we asked about August Bartolozzi?"

Woody shook his head. "I never did know his name."

"How'd it happen?" Jack asked.

Woody looked at us for a minute, then turned back to the lake. "Franklin called me one night. You knew it was him, I guess. My brother Franklin."

"Yeah," I said. Jack gave me a strange look, and I realized that he was just putting the pieces together.

"He called me. Said he was hurt bad. Told me to come to Frisco and get him. I told him to call a doctor, but he said he couldn't. Said he'd robbed a bank. I told Momma I was going catfishing. She'd had a real bad heart attack just awhile before. I figured if I told her about Franklin, it'd finish her right there."

He looked toward us as if we had asked a question. I nodded my head, and he went on. "So I drove to Frisco and located this place where he said he was. But he was dead when I got there. Been shot. Him and another guy. Both of 'em dead. I didn't know what to do. First I was gonna call the cops, but then I thought about Momma. What do you think would have happened if she'd found out Franklin had been killed sticking up a bank?"

"It would have been pretty rough," Jack said.

Woody nodded and looked down at his hands. He seemed to be finished.

I still wasn't satisfied. After waiting for a minute or two, I asked, "So what did you do?"

"I loaded him into the back of the pickup," Woody said. "Covered him up with a tarp. Threw in anything else I could find around there. There were some guns and three or four license plates. I didn't want anybody tracing anything back to Franklin. Then I took a rag and wiped off everything in the place. Didn't want any fingerprints around. Then I drove home." He pulled at the brim of his hat and started to get up.

"Then what?" I asked.

"Took all night to get home. It was almost daylight when I got here. I carried him down to the docks and loaded him in a boat. Then I grabbed the first thing I could find to sink him. An old beat-up outboard. And I headed for the middle of the lake. But there were a couple of guys fishing out there. So I came up this way and ducked into the cove where nobody'd see me. I never thought about the lake getting low."

"Probably never happen again," Jack said.

Woody stood up and brushed off his pants. "I was afraid it'd kill Momma, see? Doctors didn't give her much time anyway. So at Christmas I sent her some flowers with Franklin's name on them, and then the next spring I sent her a telegram saying he had a job overseas."

"And you've been sending stuff ever since?" Jack asked.

Woody nodded. "Never thought it'd go on this long, but Momma's a tough one."

"How do you send telegrams from overseas?" I asked him.

Woody smiled for the first time. "Old Albert at the bus station takes care of it. He's got the Western Union setup for Los Cedros. He doesn't know about Franklin being dead, of course. Just thinks he's gone off somewhere."

"Was there a lot of money?" Jack asked. "From the bank, I mean?"

"I don't know," Woody said. "It went into the lake with the rest of the stuff."

Jack looked my way. I knew what he was thinking.

Woody walked toward his boat, then turned back toward us. His right hand was inside his jacket. "I was worried about Momma, see? Even now, I don't think she could take it if she found out what happened." He slowly brought his hand out of his jacket. He was holding a long-barreled pistol.

"Wait a minute!" Jack yelled.

18

Woody looked down at the pistol. "I didn't know what to expect when I saw that note. Figured I better not take any chances."

"I'm glad we got everything straightened out," Jack said.

I shifted around and got my feet under me. When Woody started to raise the pistol, I figured the time for talking was over. I took off running along the shoreline.

Behind me the pistol went off. I veered away from the lake and dashed uphill toward the trees, leaping over rocks and half-buried driftwood.

"Eddie!" Jack yelled.

I kept running.

"Eddie, you idiot!"

I glanced back over my shoulder. Jack and Woody were still standing beside the lake.

"Get back down here," Jack yelled. "He was just signaling."

I came down a lot more slowly than I went up.

"I wish I had a movie of that," Jack said. "You took off like you were shot out of a cannon."

"Yeah, yeah." I knew I'd be hearing about that one for a long time.

A boat was headed our way, the nose riding high out of the water. I recognized the blue and white hull of the sheriff's inboard. "It's Vince," Jack said. "Woody brought him along."

Woody turned toward me with a look I'd never seen on his face before. "I'd never hurt you, Eddie. Not for anything."

"I just went a little crazy," I said.

"I wish I had a movie," Jack said again.

Vince kept his boat at full throttle until the last second. Then he cut the engine and let the boat glide up to the bank beside our aluminum job. Vince put his hands behind his head and leaned back in the seat. "What's going on?"

"Everything's okay now," Woody said.

"Not everything," Vince said. "Jackie, I ought to kick you right into the lake. Where do you come off telling stories to your old buddy Vince? Looking for Model As, he says."

"I was an idiot," Jack said. "I'm sorry."

"Big deal. We've got a jail full of guys that are sorry. What else did you find besides that license?"

"A skeleton."

"Which you forgot to mention when you asked about the license?"

"I thought it was my dad."

Vince leaned over the steering wheel and pointed a

stubby finger at Jack. "Let's hear it from the beginning."

Jack told him the whole story, from finding the outboard to looking through the old newspapers. Woody stood and stared out at the lake. I don't think he was listening.

"You boys are a real pair." Vince shook his head, then spit in the lake. "Not a lick of sense between you." He reached over and hit the starter. His engine came to life with a growl. "As far as I'm concerned, nothing happened today. And anything that happened ten years ago is history. That's what the statute of limitations is all about. I don't want to hear about any of this again. If I do, I'll be all over you boys like fleas on a dog."

"Thanks, Vince," Jack said.

"Don't try to buddy me around, Jackie. I'm still mad at you for lying to me." He shifted into reverse, and the boat moved slowly backward. "But if you were to apologize and buy me a cinnamon roll in the morning, I think I'd get over it."

"See you then," Jack said.

The three of us stood and watched Vince go tearing out of the cove. I picked up my rod and started messing with my line so that I wouldn't have to look at Woody.

"I guess I'd better get back," Woody said, stepping into his boat.

I shoved the boat free. "I'm sorry about sending the note."

"No harm done." He started his engine and went off without looking at us again.

I picked up my rod and cast my lure far out into the lake.

"Just think," Jack said, sitting down on the bank. "Somewhere down there is a bagful of money."

I let my lure sink for a count of ten, then began to retrieve it. "Maybe there'll be another drought some day."

"Old Detective Eddie," Jack said. "It's a good thing one of us was thinking straight. I sure wasn't."

"At least you didn't go running up the hill thinking Woody was going to kill you."

Jack shook his head. "Woody. Grandma Woody. What made you think of him anyway?"

I cast out my lure again. "Last night when you were talking to Julie about people looking out for their mothers, I suddenly thought of Woody. And once I got started in that direction, all sorts of things cropped up. Nobody'd seen Franklin for years. All they had were telegrams. Why not a letter or a phone call? They've got telephones in Arabia. And everybody says Franklin was a spoiled brat. It seemed funny for a spoiled brat to be sending flowers and presents."

"I should have seen it," Jack said.

"The clincher for me was that TV set Opal got last Christmas. Opal's old set went on the blink in December, and right away Franklin sent her a new set for Christmas. Now, how would a guy in Arabia know she needed a new TV?"

"I'm feeling dumber by the minute."

I reeled in my lure. "You know what I don't understand? I don't see why Woody didn't just buy his mom a TV? Why make her think it came from Franklin?"

Jack shrugged. "Maybe he knew she'd like it better that way."

"People are crazy," I said.

"Except for me and you. And I'm not too sure about you."

"I'm serious. Just think about some of the things we found out about people. The whole world is nuts."

Jack grinned. "And the guy saying all this is going to take a thirty-mile bicycle ride tomorrow so he can spend a little time with his girlfriend's father."

On the ride back Jack leaned forward and gave me a shove. "Hotshot detectives like us—I'll bet we could locate my old man if we tried."

"You really want to find him?"

"Not right now. I've done without him for nine years. I can go awhile longer."

"That's good," I said. "We probably couldn't do it anyhow."

"You know what we ought to do?" Jack said after a minute. "We ought to start a guide service."

"What?"

"We can take people out on weekends, show 'em where to fish, bait their hooks—the whole bit. And we'll get my mom to pack big beautiful lunches."

"What if they don't catch anything?"

"We should be able to find some action for them. Besides, if they get a boat ride and some good food, they won't even care."

I shook my head. "Remember that when they ask for their money back."

"What do you think, Eddie? You ready to try the guide business?"

"Why not?" I said. "It's got to be better than the detective business."

When we chugged into the marina, Woody was out on the docks by the gas pumps. "Any luck?" he called to us.

I turned my thumbs down.

We tied up our boat and carried our rods and tackle boxes down the dock. Pooch came hustling out of the store. "Let's see all the fish."

"Didn't keep any," I told him.

He laughed. "That's the same line old Woodrow was trying to peddle. He went out this afternoon too. He was going to show me up, see? And he got skunked."

"Next time we'll bring along a camera," I said, moving past him.

"Wait a second, Eddie." Pooch stepped inside the store and came back with a 3 Musketeers bar. "Take this up to Opal, will you? Tell her I said it was sweets for the sweet."

"You'd better pay for that thing," Woody called.

Pooch laughed. "Now, Woodrow, you know my credit's good."

"Your money's better," Woody said.

Jack and I tramped across the aluminum walkway. "I feel good," I said. "I feel really good."

"Me too," Jack said. "Maybe we ought to do some real fishing tomorrow."

"I can't. My history of the marina paper is due on Monday. I have to get it done before I go over to Wendy's."

Jack sighed. "I feel sorry for a guy that lets homework get in the way of fishing."

"You know what really makes me mad?" I said. "I'm having trouble stretching out my paper to make five pages, and I have to leave out the most interesting stuff."

"Look at that," Jack shouted, pointing up the hill. A cloud of black smoke was rising above the parking lot.

The Batt brats were on the rampage again.

About the Author

P. J. PETERSEN was born in Santa Rosa, California, and grew up on a farm in Sonoma County. He attended Stanford University, San Francisco State University, and the University of New Mexico, from which he holds a doctorate in English. He lives with his wife and two daughters in Redding, California, where he teaches English at Shasta College.

This is P. J. Petersen's eighth novel. *Would You Settle for Improbable?* and *Nobody Else Can Walk It for You* both were American Library Association Best Books for Young Adults.